The Allegra Series

The Allegra Series

a novel by
Barbara Lambert

Porcepic Books
an imprint of

Beach Holme Publishing
Vancouver

This book is published by Beach Holme Publishing, #226—2040 West 12th Ave., Vancouver, BC, V6J 2G2. This is a Porcepic Book.

We acknowledge the financial support of the Canada Council for the Arts, the Government of Canada through the Book Publishing Industry Development Program (BPIDP) and the assistance of the Province of British Columbia through the British Columbia Arts Council for our publishing activities and program.

THE CANADA COUNCIL | LE CONSEIL DES ARTS
FOR THE ARTS | DU CANADA
SINCE 1957 | DEPUIS 1957

Editor: Joy Gugeler
Cover Design: Teresa Bubela
Type Design: Jen Hamilton
Cover Art: John William Waterhouse, '*I am Half-Sick of Shadows,*' said The *Lady of Shalott*, 1915. 39$^{1/2}$" x 29", oil on canvas. Art Gallery of Ontario, Toronto. Gift of Mrs. Phillip B. Jackson, 1971. Used with permission.
Author photo: Shaena Lambert
Line Art: Lorna Schwenk

Canadian Cataloguing in Publication Data

Lambert, Barbara Rose,
  The Allegra series

  ISBN 0-88878-399-X

  I. Title.
PS8573.A3849A84 1999   C813'.54   C99-910885-9
PR9199.3.L2849A84 1999

For Linda

Contents

June

*T*he pull of clay is a mystery, until you have its gritty substance in your hands, feel it move, feel the lure of the red earth, the danger. As you work it, one of you will change. First it will mark you, mark your hands and all your clothes, fill your house with sifting layers of its presence as it dries. Then it will invade your sleep. Already your palms are red as those of any eastern bride....

§

Mona Lindhall sits in a cavernous warehouse gallery in Toronto, surrounded by the stern terracotta shapes of her recent installation. The table before her is piled with books on myth, ancient music, the history of clay, the origin of cloth. She was once told a story she now recalls as just a tantalizing thread of antique lore. If only she can find it again, it will lead her to the heart of her new work, which will involve not just clay but also story, song, brilliant fabric, painted banners, or kites. Or feathered wings.

Tonight she is entangled in a curious and opinionated volume that rises above the rest. *Web and Fire: A Brief History of Cloth and Clay.* As a street lamp sheds yellow light on the street outside, and the old building on Spadina wheezes with its burden of hot summer air, Mona skips to a chapter entitled "The Secret Life of String."

℘

...In which we intend to go right back to that moment when someone needed to tie a lover to a tree and found herself rolling a few stalks of flax on her naked thigh, thus forming a thick and flexible piece of twine....

Or cast back to the time of two other lovers....The most famous length of string in classic myth must be that which Daedalus handed Ariadne, so she could help Theseus find his way to the centre of the labyrinth and back again.

The comparison of the human life-span to a thread is very old, "span" deriving from the verb "to spin." With that thread hadn't Ariadne literally given Theseus the gift of life? As he stumbled down twisted corridors, following the roars of that creature half man, half bull, a numbing sense of obligation may have seeped to him down that long silken filament. Why else would he have abandoned Ariadne on Naxos? Why would anyone desert the one who had led them to the centre, and safely out again?

Later on Naxos, an odd cult sprang up, a cult of Aphrodite and Ariadne combined, in which a young man was chosen to go through the sounds and contortions of giving birth, as part of the yearly rites of spring....

June

℘

Brad Lindhall dragged Mona's art supplies up from the basement, all the charcoal and paper and half-squeezed oils from before she seized on clay. He meant to throw everything away, but the texture of the paper held him back. He came upon at least a hundred sheets of Carlyle Japan, creamy, with deckled edges. The wastefulness, the negligence, the value of everything that she had just abandoned, pitched him into a state of liberation. The slim bundle of charcoal he had been on the verge of snapping like a wrist-bone pulled him in.

On many nights after that, when his son slept his precarious young sleep, Brad sat in the kitchen, the door half open to Nicky's room. He began drawing funnel shapes. He had no idea what attracted him to these, but he was thrilled to coax the black into an impression of a long black tube. Around the funnels he drew the kitchen table, the sink, the stove. Mona had baked her vegetarian lasagna at that stove. Also chocolate brownies (which he had sometimes caught her eating straight from the pan).

He drew the hooked rug in the background too, wrinkled the way it had been after they made love there, the night that Nicholas was conceived. She had been slicing mushrooms for pasta, that earthy dark-finned taste still on her tongue. When Brad got down on his knees and slid his tongue down her stomach to her own dark and finny area, for once she abandoned care and let him bring her down and down onto the old hooked rug that had a pattern of a garden gate and foxgloves, a thatched cottage in behind. Around the humps and wrinkles of the rug he drew squares of black and white tile. In painting after painting, he set down this domestic geometry—cupboards of yellow, bright as sun, and above the sink a stained-glass window he had discovered at an auction.

Double vision had afflicted him since Mona left, his old life almost tangible under the transparency of his present circumstance. Her voice slid out from the folds of burlap curtains in the living room, from the shadows underneath corners of papers on his desk, from the hollows of mugs on the pinewood dresser.

He had no idea what the empty circles at the end of his funnels might eventually reveal. He did not mention this obsessive work to Mona, when she called.

§

Before the written word, in epic times, the glorious history of the tribe was woven into "story cloths." These were the work of the princesses and queens. Battles were what these noble women recorded: battles among giants, battles among their godly ancestors. Yet on the most ancient excavated sites what we find are loom weights, bobbins, shards of terracotta cooking pots, not weapons. There was life, before war. First came clay. Then came cloth. Small wonder that Athena was the patron of weaving as well as war. She managed to have it all, worshiped by the Athenians as the goddess of fertility, the protector of the city, the guardian of shipbuilders, the one able to calm the sea god, by pouring oil upon the waters.

§

One day Brad came home from Acme Glass to find a letter from Mona, ripe with recrimination. If he hadn't known her better he might have supposed she'd been drinking, but he suspected it had more to do with her work. She accused him of forcing her to have his child, said it was his fault that she had almost killed Nicky that time he had cried and cried until she had slammed him in his crib and gone down to the basement to work, turning up the music so she couldn't hear him. When she finally went to him he had burrowed down to the foot of the crib, his head underneath the blankets. He could hardly breathe.

Maybe she would come home, Mona said. Maybe she would give it all up and come home and face what she had done.

He had seen her in this state when her work wasn't going well. Last spring, she dug up their whole front yard and planted squash, tomatoes, pumpkins, ornamental cabbages with ragged purple frills. "The tigers have disappeared from the forests of Vietnam," she'd told him when he came home and found her digging fiercely, "the elephants, as well. How can you ask why I would want to do this?" She had been working on a show of tea pots for a small craft gallery. She had opened the kiln that morning to find that half of them had cracked. Still it was all he could do, now, to keep from going to the phone and saying "Yes. Come home."

That night when he gave Nicky his bath, it struck him, as his son slipped and squealed between his hands, that for almost six months he hadn't really *seen* him.

"Daddy, don't!"

"Don't what?"

"Don't do that with your eyes."

Don't stare.

"Come on then, let's rinse off this shampoo."

Nicky lay back, completely trusting, in water deep enough to drown in, his head cupped in Brad's hand. The pale translucence of his skin. His mother's skin. Though the smell of Mona's skin was hot and dry, not milky like her child's. How cruel that Brad could still smell the hot dry climate of the hollow of her throat, when she was more than half a continent away.

The bath water was so deep that Nicky was almost floating. "Is the soap out?" he said, his eyes still tightly shut. Brad lowered his hand. The water rose around Nicky's ears, to the edges of his eyes, then his eyes flicked open (black eyes with points of light; his mother's eyes) and he reached out and grabbed Brad's arm.

"Dad! You almost let me go!"

Brad had trouble settling into his work, after that. He got up from the kitchen table and walked downstairs. Across Mona's darkened studio, past the lumpy shapes of two potter's wheels, her pug-mill, some abandoned sacks of clay, he could see the lights of West Vancouver on the far side of the inlet, the mountains looming against the glow cast upward by the city. He could see his wife, too, so clearly now. She had chopped her hair off just months before she left, wore it all brushed forward in little strands around her face, so that—taking into consideration her sharp commanding nose—she'd looked a bit like Napoleon as she stood at her work bench wedging clay. She was wearing jeans, an old blue tank top. Her arms were smudged, her muscles throbbed. He saw her, he smelled her; the empty basement filled with the warmth of clay as it turned to dust on her arms. Her words echoed with a ferocity that almost made him smile.

"Brad, it's all completely organized. The collective has a day care. Nicky will get more stimulation than while I've been with him trying to work at home."

"Who's going to pay? Don't tell me your grant covers it!"

"I'm going to talk to my father on the weekend."

June

Brad climbed the stairs from the basement and wandered around his echoing house. He stood for a long time at his front window, looking out at the shadows thrown by the street light, the leafy silhouettes of chestnut branches waving on the sidewalk, the humps and hollows of his yard. He had done almost nothing to it since she left.

At Mona's parents' place that weekend, the discussion going round and round, Brad had looked out another window to see little Nicky running backwards toward the beach.

"I don't know what all this useless talk is about! If Mona goes to Toronto, fine. But my boy stays with me!" he shouted before he dashed out and snatched up his son.

Now he stood with his palms against the glass, staring at his reflection as if to draw something from its square of coolness.

Yet glass is made of sand. A dry fact and a mystery.

When he settled at the table, the light above seemed blue-white, fluorescent, though it was a mellow Chinese paper globe. Little by little, the drawing pulled him in. He shifted his chair across the room, pinned a paper to the board, began a study of the room from an entirely different angle, sketched the pinewood dresser and his mother's Mammy-jar (which in a brilliant jab of wickedness she had left to Mona in her will). He was working with a broad-tipped felt pen, moving around the contours of the jar's grinning head. Look at that shine, the glisten of that cheek, the highlights, the reflection of the paper lamp, now the rhythmic strokes on patterned wood....

The phone rang. His hand jumped. The sketch ruined.

§

The Greeks say the first woman on earth was Pandora. Zeus commissioned an Olympian potter to create her out of clay as vengeance upon man and his benefactor Prometheus for the gift of fire. Aphrodite's task, Hesiod tells us, was to "shed grace upon Pandora's head," while Athena's was to teach her to weave. After that the gods were ordered to endow Pandora with every charm, including curiosity and deceit, before she was sent as wife to the simple brother of Prometheus, who made her the gift of a beautiful carved chest, but told her never to open it.

§2

"Is that Brad Lindhall by any chance?" The voice on the phone had a green and pleasant quality, like lettuce. "Have I got you at a bad time? Shall I call you back? This is Allegra Schliemann, I don't know if you remember me. Mona told me that you sometimes work on the side? Of course that was ages ago now."

"It depends on the job," Brad said.

"I was wondering if you'd like to come over and give me a quote to put in a window. I live in co-op housing, where, sadly, there are rules. I should have a view over English Bay, and instead I've just got this view of Burrard Bridge. If I go out on my balcony and crane over the side, I get a glimpse of a quarter inch of sea. But if I had a corner window, I could see right across to Bowen Island. Unfortunately any renovations have to go through numerous committees," she was saying, "so what I need is someone who can think 'creatively'. Could you come and take a look?"

"I can't make any promises but I'll drop by sometime next week."

"When do you think you could make it?"

"I said, sometime next week."

June

"But when? I need to arrange to be here when you come."

"I'll give you a call."

"Did I get it wrong? You don't do windows?"

"Okay," he found himself saying, though he had no idea how he would fit it in, "I'll drop around tomorrow then, between twelve and twelve-fifteen." He hung up the phone.

§

The Odyssey tells us that when Alkandre the wife of Polybos of Thebes entertained Helen of Troy, she presented Helen with fine gifts, including a golden spindle and a gold-rimmed silver wool-basket with wheels. Archaeological evidence supports the legend. Golden spindles have been found in tombs dating as far back as the Early Bronze Age, in Turkey for example, where a woman decked in gold and precious stones clasped a spindle much like that described by Homer. There is even a scholar who argues that the Venus de Milo was spinning, before she lost her arms.

The Fates themselves were referred to as The Spinners by the Greeks. They spoke of Clotho who spun the thread of life, and Lachesis who measured it out. And the one who chose when to cut it off, whose name was Atropos.

§

He had always wondered what this place was like, Seaview Terrace. The designers had done an imaginative job of preserving half a dozen of the west end's distinctive wooden houses—gabled, trimmed with filigree—and had echoed that motif in the concrete apartment towers behind. A metal gate closed the area off from the busy street. He climbed red brick steps flanked by ferns and salal shiny with rain. Allegra Schliemann was in the middle tower. He crossed a wide brick terrace, headed for the glassed-in elevator chute. As he rode up to the sixth floor he tried to envision her.

A woman a good decade older than Brad opened the door, teetering on two canes. She was almost as tall as he was, with the kind of bones that held her very straight despite the walking sticks, and waist-length black hair that reminded him of an Egyptian drawing, the straight blunt way it fell. Her eyes were green.

"Am I glad to see you," she said. She pushed the door wider with one of her canes, then gave a flick of her head toward the living room. She wore black leather pants, a long black t-shirt pulled in by a belt, silver hoops, and a small gold locket. She had broad streaks of white in her hair.

He trailed her into the main room. The kitchen was separated by half a dozen wooden coat-trees with lengths of brightly-coloured fabric hanging from their branches, suspended by metal loops and chains. Beyond that was a large central table heaped with more fabric, and a sitting area by the window, a curtained alcove to the side. The window had a good view of the bridge, that was true, and strings of cars sloshing through rain. He brushed against one of the coat trees and the chains skittered off, the brass rings rolling across the floor.

"Oh, don't worry...!" She laughed as Brad tried to re-hang the fabric pieces. "Just dump them here. They're for a project I'm developing. I'm afraid this whole place is.... Well, you can see."

The room was chaotic, but it had a lush feel about it too, plants everywhere, vines climbing around the window, in the corner a cascading spider fern.

"But you don't remember me, do you?" she said. "You came

by the studio once, with Mona...." She looked hesitant. "FibreWorks. Down on Cordova."

Mona had taken him to all sorts of craft places on weekends; he *did* remember a studio with woven shawls, coats, yardage and pottery for sale. He remembered thinking the building ought to have been condemned. He studied Allegra Schliemann again, sliding one image over the other, making adjustments, thinking of the dark-haired woman who had come from the back room that day. How long ago had it actually been? Those streaks of white in her hair. He recalled Mona talking about her, saying she had become mysteriously sick—had left the man she worked with to go off to the Gulf Islands with her doctor. Brad had felt queasy listening to Mona recall Allegra's string of love affairs.

"We're changing the whole place, FibreWorks, now," Allegra explained. "We're going into the production of printed cloth, so I'm using this as my design studio while all of that is going on. Light is crucial. Now that's where I want my window—there." She pointed a cane at the corner where a large African carving loomed.

It wasn't light that was crucial; the place was so full of *things*. As he followed her to the corner he stumbled over one of the carpets.

"Jesus."

"Sorry. Are you okay? This place is ridiculous, but I don't have anywhere else to store these at the moment. I'm trying to move, but you know how that is." She turned and looked quizzically at him. "*Do* you know how that is?"

"I've only lived in three places my whole life."

"Really? A well-rooted person. I don't know many of those." She was half frowning, her head tilted. "I'm a bit scattered and into floor-filing, as you can see," pointing to an arrangement of gourd-shaped containers and a collection of primitive black stone sculptures. Along another wall was a low couch piled with cushions: woven, printed, or thick with embroidery and small winking mirrors. Baskets teetered upon baskets. She needed carpentry not windows, a clear floor, order, shelves.

"You have enough here to start an import business."

"I was going to do that, once. These rugs were supposed to be the start." She leaned back against the arm of a carved wooden chair, almost a throne. "We got them when we were on the way home from Nigeria. My husband and I were traveling through Turkey, backpacking, and fell in love with these in a shop in a bazaar, so we bargained and bargained…"

Her voice had a lulling effect. As he listened to her talk, he composed the scene in his mind.

"Patrick and I kept going back to the same shop, day after day," she said, "discussing the price, until finally the owner came down to what we had originally offered. I think he liked our persistence. So there we were with a dozen carpets we had to trust him to send back to Canada. Patrick thought we'd never see them again."

Too much of a doubter, Patrick.

"Don't you have storage in the basement?" Brad pictured a floor-to-ceiling closet neatly dividing the room, started measuring the space in his head.

"Sure. This is just the tip of the iceberg. I have things stored at the studio, too, and over on Hornby Island, where I lived briefly."

She was staring at him. He felt himself colour.

"Good heavens, you must be starved," she said. "No, no, no, it's too late to get out of it. It's all prepared. Don't look so alarmed."

Before he could say anything she shuffled across the room,

quite painfully now, on her two canes, shifting things around on the cluttered table, starting to clear off a space. The room was chilly; a door was open to the balcony. Dank unseasonable air seeped in, the sound of the rain.

"Do you mind if I close that door?"

"Oh. Go ahead. It's just that I have trouble with the heat, these days."

She pulled at the neck of her black shirt, as if the room was stifling. "Now if you go into the fridge, you'll find a couple of platters," she said, an edge to her voice. He opened the fridge and saw two large ceramic plates: fruit, vegetables, quivering tofu and dense black bread, all cut into the shapes of stars.

"Do you think this is ridiculous?" She was half squinting at him, her head to the side. "Of course you do. You see I bought a new gadget. Look at this, it can cut things into any shape you want. My hands don't do that kind of thing on their own anymore. I was thinking that I could adapt it to cut fabric. Now, in the drawer closest to the fridge are a couple of serving forks."

The serving forks were heavy silver, elaborately carved. They almost slipped through her fingers as he handed them to her. "Shall I do that?" he asked.

"No, I have a plan."

He watched her trying to lift the star-shaped pieces of food. Her hands didn't shake; they were slim-fingered, they looked strong, but they didn't want to do what they were told. She fiddled about, trying to arrange a constellation that pleased her.

He had to get back to work. "Come on," he said, trying to keep the impatience from his voice, "let me do that."

"Okay. Sure." She handed him the implements. "I suppose you're wondering what ails me?"

A blob of tofu slid off the fork and hit his knee. He could feel it oozing through the rip in his jeans. Her eyes were so engaging, yet he felt like such a brute. He stopped serving to give her the attention she deserved.

"They seem to have decided on MS," she said, "but then they say things like 'the most we can do is draw a pattern' and what they draw is pretty bleak. I've decided to figure a way out of this myself."

"You're very open about it."

Brad had an urge to reach out and rearrange the way she held herself, hide certain details, but when she smiled her disfigurement slid from view.

"That's the worst thing about being sick. People think you ought to go around with a paper bag over your head so they don't have to see you."

"I didn't mean...."

"No, I didn't mean to accuse you. But it *can* be exhausting, trying to spare the sensibilities of the healthy."

There was something generous about the way she opened up the door and let him walk right in, describing the progression of her illness, the way it had began with just a numbness, a tingling in her feet. In any case, she was on the path to recovery. He was unexpectedly sympathetic when she got back to the plans for the windows.

"Look," he said, "I'd have to do this through the office, no matter what. It poses a lot of problems. For one thing we're, what, on the seventh floor? With a sheer drop below? It calls for special equipment. They'd have to pass it for safety, Worker's Compensation, all that."

"Oh, sure," she said. "Naturally. But how much can it cost, to punch a couple windows through a wall? It doesn't look complicated."

"It's not a small job."

"Still you could give me a ball-park figure, couldn't you? Something the board wouldn't turn down out of hand. And if the cost crept up a bit...?"

§ɔ

Shortly after the invention of weaving women began to stamp designs on cloth, first using gourds, then shapes carved out of clay, quickly coming to terms with the demands of Pattern, which still holds us in its thrall. Who hasn't lain in bed and tried to discern the pattern of the wallpaper—that flower repeated here, there turned the other way around—or followed the path of those twining vine leaves, counted clusters of grapes. Repetition and variation. Pattern's essential elements.

One quality that keeps a pattern lively is caprice: "unaccountable change of mind or conduct" as the Oxford tells us: also "work of sportive fancy in art."

Here we see the power of negative space, the way a design can flip so that the background leaps forward. Consider the ground beneath the fallen bloom, the forest between the leaves. Consider the jester in sportive fancy, the tiny bells like upturned tears.

§ɔ

Brad was back at Allegra's place the next day with a written estimate. She wasn't home. He put the envelope through her mail slot and phoned that night to make sure that she had received it.

"I'll have to ask you to leave a message," her voice said on the machine. "You know what to do." He hung up before the tone. The same thing happened the next day, and the next. He felt a bit unsettled, a bit absurd.

"Where have you been?" he demanded when he reached her.

She laughed. "What do you mean?"

"I called and called. Did you leave the city?"

"Oh what a shame. My machine must be on the blink again. I didn't get your message. But listen, I'm sorry I didn't get back to you about the estimate. I'm afraid things have been wild."

"Anyway, I had an idea," he said.

"Really?"

"I thought maybe I could come over and show it to you."

"You can't tell me on the phone?"

"Well, it's...."

"How about sometime tomorrow?"

"Sunday. That's the only day I really have to spend with Nicky."

"Right. Your little boy. So next week then," she said. "What day are you free?"

℘

There are many timeless pattern motifs: the tree of life, the stepped zigzag, the key meander, the lotus. And of course the maze.

The tree of life has been with us from Biblical times, represented first as little more than a stick, though often flanked by griffins or lions. In Babylonia it grew into an ornate fan.

The Greeks had their sacred groves. In India sacred trees even married.

Ritual mazes have been found scratched on stones by primitive societies all over the world.

ʂ

It took Brad five trips on the elevator just to bring up all the glass.

"What is this?" Allegra demanded, laughing. "What's going on?"

"Hang on. I'll have to arrange this so you can see for yourself."

"Look, I'm an artist. I can visualize."

"Well I'm an artist too." He was amazed that this had slipped out, yet strangely he found himself turning on her. "I don't look like an artist?"

"I'd say you were a mad environmentalist, a boy scout gone wild." She reached up and touched his face, traced his features, filled them in. "You've got those eyes, and such a nose. Also the widest mouth I've ever seen."

July

During work or after work, that week and the next, Brad covered two of Allegra's walls with mirrored glass, the doors of her closets too. He put a mirrored screen out on her balcony to catch the waters of the inlet, the far shore, the ships that bobbed at anchor so that even as she sat working at her table she could be wrapped in view.

Allegra gave him an extra set of keys in case she couldn't be there when he came by.

On the first day of the project, he arrived to find her in a wheelchair. She tried to open the door wide enough to let him through, her chair half-blocking the way.

She wheeled to the table, pushing the chair with difficulty over the rucked-up rug.

"I almost went without all the gear I'll need for the studio." She unhooked a large Mexican bag from the side of her chair and started putting in tracing paper, scissors, a metal candy box full of pens.

"We're designing placemats. To keep some money coming in, until the printing operation gets going. I'll show you the next time you're over. Here, could you hang this on the back?"

Having accomplished all that, she didn't seem to be leaving after all. She watched him as he took off his jacket, as he tried to place his tools without knocking something over.

"As you are here, could you give me a hand downstairs? I'm running late."

"You're not going to wheel all the way to Cordova Street?"

"No. My car's in the basement. But the way this building is designed, it's not easy to manage all the fire doors."

"There's got to be a better way," he said, when she finally settled into the driver's seat after he'd helped her down the elevator and through several sets of heavy metal doors. He didn't understand how she could have managed on her own.

"You should conserve your energy."

"In other words, stay home?"

"At least take taxis."

"I don't think you understand my situation. I've had to quit weaving for a while because I don't have the strength or the manual dexterity anymore, so I'm changing the direction of the studio. A lot of people are pitching in, but at the moment none of us takes out what you'd call a living wage."

He found himself looming over her, leaning in the door. "You could take a lot of taxis for what it costs to license this car."

Her green eyes were flecked with brown. "It is very import...
to me," she told him, "to be able to get around independently."

$\wp$

That morning as he worked her phone rang and rang, her machine
clicked on and off. There'd been an article in the paper concerning
her new venture. Friends called with congratulations, or offered to
help. Brad wondered how she found so many willing volunteers.
After an hour or so of this, he pulled the cord.

She returned late in the afternoon. He heard the thud of her
wheelchair as she bumped open her front door. "Oh, you're here,"
she said, "and look how much you've done." She made a long and
silent inspection of the half-completed mirrored wall to the left of
her balcony door. He'd had to patch it together out of left-overs
from a dormered bedroom he'd finished on an Acme contract
months ago.

"Brad, this is remarkable. I don't know what to say."

She moved to the kitchen, bags from the market swinging on
the back of her chair. She started unloading the contents: a
barbecued chicken, salads, a bottle of Okanagan wine. "I hoped
that you'd be able to stay and have a bite. Can you? Or do you have
to get home to your little boy?"

Brad realized he hadn't stopped to eat his sandwich, he'd been
so determined to get something significant accomplished before
she returned. "I'll call Mrs. Chan. Perhaps she can stay and give
Nicky his dinner."

She busied herself clearing the table while he set things up with
Mrs. Chan. She located a tablecloth friends had sent her from Bali

and stopped to tell him about the trip. She set him on a hunt for matching napkins in a drawer beneath the bed.

"It's not so easy for me now, to get down on my knees."

The curtains that closed off the sleeping area were made of lumpy white wool, but when he pulled them, they were lined with huge red poppies. The bed, which took up the whole curtained space, was covered in a smaller print of the same colours. He felt odd, kneeling in that intimate enclosure, folding back the flowery quilt, rooting around beneath patterned cushions, silky cotton sheets.

Allegra was in the kitchen, melting the bottoms of candles so they'd stand upright in a pottery candelabra she bought in Tuscany.

"I have to get back there before too long," she told him, pausing to embark on an itinerary of foreign-sounding names, describing a trail she'd once hiked, "...and it leads you right past the place where St. Francis received the stigmata. So beautiful those woods, scrub-oak, and chestnuts hung with spiky golden balls...but it's rugged walking; it's much wilder than I'd imagined, that part of Italy."

"How would you manage that now?" The question more blunt than he'd intended.

"I'm going to get better. Now come on. Sit down."

The chicken was moist, tender, and still warm, and the salad contained raisins, pine-nuts, goat cheese, frizzy bits of lettuce. He refilled his wine and looked around at the room. It had grown cave-like in the dark, the candles flickering, while the mirrors caused the space to expand. He got up and pulled open the curtain, looked out at the bridge and the ships moored in the bay. The lights made Chinese writing in the water, reflected passages into the room.

℘

Brad changed his arrangement with Mrs. Chan. She would be prepared to stay on and give Nicky his supper, in case he couldn't get home from Allegra's in time.

"This must be a very important job," Mrs. Chan said. "I've never known you to do so much work, at night."

"I'm lucky it came up. I need the money."

"Every time you're away he asks for macaroni," Mrs. Chan said.

℘

It was a hot night. Brad was only half listening. She was wearing a dark red dress the same colour as the wine in her glass, low at the neck. When she leaned toward him he caught the vapour of her moist, hot skin.

How would he convey this in paint, the ruby glint of the dress, the glisten of the skin?

"If we don't make changes ourselves," she said, "some other force does it for us, not necessarily the changes we'd hoped for. Do you know Escher's drawings? That print of the fish turning into birds? I believe we all have that ability, if we could tap it. Imagine rising from the water for the first time, filling your lungs with air. I'd like to design *that* pattern in fabric."

"You make patterns out of everything," he said, noting the near completion of the mirrors. He poured them both another glass of wine. She needed a better arrangement in the kitchen: a chopping block that would hinge outward, so that she could sit as she worked.

"Then there's the story of Diana, the goddess of the hunt," she said. "A young man was hunting with his pack of hounds, dogs so swift they could chase anything, and he came upon a goddess bathing naked in a stream. He stood and looked at her, which you might imagine was a reasonable thing to do. But she threw some drops of water in his face and he turned into a stag. His dogs could smell his fear. They ran him down and tore him to pieces. He was eaten by his own faithful servants."

She watched him expectantly.

"I hate stories like that," he said. "I hate suspecting there is something going on behind your back, something you'll never know until it's too late."

"You're a bit defensive."

"I've just never liked those sort of fables."

"I think this one reveals a basic human truth though. We have these qualities—maybe thrift, maybe the desire to get ahead, or..." she broke off, "yes, even something like my determination to get well. And we think we have them in check, but if we're not careful, they can turn on us just like that, and we will be devoured."

"The fatal flaw."

"No, I think it's more like the fatal virtue."

Allegra pushed back from the table and reached for her canes. She made her way to the couch, sank among her brilliant cushions.

"Listen," she said, "I've got a bit of dope, if you'll go in the fridge and bring the mustard tin. I just use it because of all of this," she said making a gesture that took in her whole body with a twist of the hand. "You'll have to roll it, though."

He came and sat beside her, held the butt for her. Her drag left it crinkled, damp at the end. The paper stuck to his lips. Brad felt the sweet touch of the drug take hold. For a moment he was in the curl at the centre of a wave, the eye of a storm. Across the room her coat trees vibrated in the draft caused by tiny explosions of falling colour, purple vibrating next to scarlet, a tumble of yellow shooting its own light into the darkening room.

"You know," Allegra said, "as my health has been worsened, one person after another has come along to help me, but actually has become dependent *on* me."

The marijuana was lifting him beautifully just an inch or so off the surface of the pillowed chesterfield.

"When I first got sick, Max was going to cart me off to Hornby to take care of me and at the same time explore that other side of himself." She sat forward and gave Brad an urgent look. "I think some people should *never* do that. Especially doctors."

"No, doctors are the worst."

"He'd always thought he would write. But he went to pieces over there. Once he got away from the city noise, he couldn't stand any noise at all. Eventually even my breathing got to him. I had to escape, finally. And now Max's wife has died and I seem to be the one he's turning to."

The two of them sat side by side, Allegra's colourful sad life washing over Brad. She had not turned the lights on and the room was lit only with the bobbing lights of cars passing over the bridge.

"Do I look like a victim to you? The worst good thing about me," she was looking straight at him, "the fatal virtue I suppose, is how I fall in love, again and again. I don't mean just with men, I mean with projects, places, paintings, ideas. And men, of course."

"No, you don't look like a victim. You look just lovely to me." The phrase hung there, winking in the lights of passing cars. She lay back on the sofa, adrift in her hair, and he thought her face had been carved exceptionally by time, and by the eyes of all those men.

§

The stories of cloth and clay and pattern are intimately bound. The first woman, as we have learned, was made of clay and then "girdled" by Athena, reminding us of the girdle of a hundred tassels that Hera borrowed from Aphrodite to seduce Zeus away from the battlefield of Troy. In fact Venus figures in terracotta, with string skirts carved over their ample forms, date back at least twenty thousand years.

In caves similar to those where such figures have been found, we have also come upon walls covered with a patterning of hand prints surely intended to have magical effect. Others show hunting scenes so powerful in their arrangement and abstraction that they remind us again of the sorcery a fine design can unleash on the world.

Ancient, too, is the understanding of a piece of cloth's practical power. Consider the Greek tale of Philomela, locked away in her high tower....

§

The following week Brad came into Allegra's apartment to surprise her while she worked at what he supposed was a variety of loom. It was hanging on the back of a tall cupboard door he had tried once and found locked. The loose threads dangling below the woven part were tied in clusters, weighted by small brass bells. These set off a tinkling alarm as she swivelled on her stool, found him looking over her shoulder.

"Yes, it's a very old type," she said. "A warp-weighted vertical loom, only portable of course, but otherwise more or less the kind of loom Penelope would have used." She was talking too fast and brightly. "You know, when she wove to keep her suitors at bay. They were insisting she should marry one of them, while she waited for Ulysses to come home. She had promised that she would choose as soon as she finished her weaving. She would weave away all day, and then tear out the design at night."

Brad glimpsed a long bulky roll of woven cloth at the top of the loom. The edge of some dark pattern extended down into the open area. In the middle of this was a surprising blotch of colour, gold and red and creamy orange—very rough—that looked like a lily or perhaps a star. "I was just fooling around a bit," she was saying as she pushed back her stool awkwardly and closed the door. "It's a tapestry I used to work on, a long on-going project. But now it's frustrating for me. I don't know why I decided to have another try at it today."

Allegra was embarrassed, but also radiant. She was wearing a scoop-necked tunic of woven silk, soft tones that blended all the colours of the clouded sea outside. In the light his mirrors threw, her skin had the paleness of women he had seen once in a book of French paintings, a whiteness that in the shadows took on oddly vibrating colour.

"I've missed you," she said. "Come see what I've been up to."

She had her new line of placemats spread out on the table in sets, ready to be taken around to stores. The mats were made with layers of felt, each layer smaller than the one below, and on top was a pattern of cut-out fruit, or flowers. "They're meant to have the look and feel of molas," she said. "That's cut-out felt work they do on an island off Panama. But these are just samples. The designs are pasted on with speed-sew. Once we are in full production they will all be appliquéed by hand, which will make them expensive. We are going all-out for the carriage trade."

She paused to take in his expression. "You're wondering why, if I'm selling to the carriage trade, I'm living like this? Believe me, so am I. But you should come down to the studio and see what I've made of that place since last you were there. The printing venture is where we are going to make our fortune. What do you say? Shall I cut you in?"

She began explaining how you could take a yard of silk you'd imported from the Orient for less than a dollar and make from it the sort of hand-rolled square that Chanel or Fendi sold for perhaps three hundred times that amount. The studio was setting up to do hand-printed yardage, both for fashion and for interior design.

"We'll be the only ones in Canada doing it," she said. "We'll be eligible for small business loans and grants. We'll be national treasures. I'm planning a collection using each of the provincial flowers, not the usual tourist thing, but a truly elegant design. In fact, look, I've got to get these placemats over to FibreWorks for Faye to package up. You remember Faye, she went to art school with Mona? Well —no don't you dare protest—you can drive me there right now."

§

Exactly as he recalled, FibreWorks was on the ground floor of a crumbling building on the lower east side, underneath the rooms of a down-and-out hotel. But inside, Allegra had painted everything—the walls, the high ceilings with carved moldings from another era, the shelves and counters of the shop in front and the long cavernous workspace in behind—a gleaming pearly white. The oak floor had been varnished to a state of amber, and the shop was filled with light. An intermittent drizzle ceased as they came in and the sun slid through the plate glass at the front, striking a line of old-fashioned apothecary bottles in the window, pooling coloured light on the floor.

"They're full of dyes," Allegra said. "Or at least that's what they represent, to give the idea that we're engaged in something like alchemy in here."

Three women came through the beaded curtain at the back of the shop. Brad recognized Faye Minot now and he remembered that he'd never liked her much, always conspiring with Mona in some way, though she was pretty, with her pointy little face and red-gold curls. The two with her were college kids, her students, a girl with green woolly hair, and a hefty blonde with a paintbrush stuck through a topknot. All three wore overalls. They were heading over to the college, for a workshop. Faye said she would return first thing in the morning, to package up the mats.

In the back room, a man slightly bigger than an upright freezer was working with a power saw. He stopped when they came through and glared. "This is Manny," Allegra said, "the person we can't get along without." She fished a pair of spectacles from her bag. "Let me see what you've been doing."

"I'm heading out for coffee," Manny said.

"I hired him from the Detox Centre up the street," Allegra explained. "Not Mr. Personality, as you see; he's had a rough time." For a moment Brad was afraid she was considering telling him all about Manny's rough life. "He hates to be interrupted. It keeps him from the jitters, to have something interesting to do."

She walked Brad down to the far end, her canes making a loud uneven noise. Manny was building a thirty-metre table so they could print the bolts of cloth. The floor was brilliant with varnish, even back here. "Though I don't suppose it will stay like this when we start the printing. It was lovely when we were weaving, to have beautiful surroundings." She opened the door to the lane. Sun glinted off the trash cans in the alley, reflected on the clumps of wild herbs and grasses hanging below the ceiling, the baskets full of dried roots and berries stacked along one wall, ingredients she'd used to make her dyes for weaving silk and wool.

"I used to have three looms in here, you know. Faye used to work with me, and other students from the college, apprenticing, that was the way I could make it pay. They all wanted to come and work here. It's a lovely thing, women working in that way, though it might seem tedious if you didn't understand it. It can take an entire day, two women working together, just warping up a pattern on a loom. I say women because that's who has traditionally done it."

"How did you start doing all this?" he said quickly.

She laughed. "Itchy feet. My wanton days of wandering. Don't ever let anybody tell you it's not worthwhile, wasting time."

"And?"

"Well it was in a little hilltown in Italy. Chiusi?" She paused, as if there were some hope that he might recognize the name. "In their marvelous museum, I saw an ancient Greek vase.... Look, do you mind if I sort out these skeins of silk while we're here? In fact you can help me. Here," she indicated a big supermarket Kleenex carton on the floor, "Manny just dumped all these in here, when he took down the shelves on the other side. I think he was having a bad day." The box was a jumble of looped and twisted shiny coloured thread. "I want to sell these. Well I have to, actually; we're a little short of capital at the moment, everything helps. So if we could just sort the skeins into piles of each colour and put those into bags? There's a stack of brown Safeway bags over there. Could you tip out the box on the table?" indicating a long work table under the herbs.

They sat across from each other there, sorting through the small mountain of beautiful shimmery colours.

"Where did you get all these?"

"Where did I get them? I dyed them." She laughed. "That's what I used to do. Don't get me going; I'll tell you all about it, if you don't watch out." She shook her head. "I miss the work, I'm afraid."

"You were about to tell me how you started weaving, though."

"Oh, right. Where was I?"

"In Italy, I think."

"Yes..." She smiled. "That remarkable vase. It was decorated with a picture of Penelope at her loom, waiting for Ulysses to come home, while her son Telemachus is facing her holding a spear, saying 'Don't marry one of those men,' though of course not prepared to fight them off; he just left it all up to her.... It is remarkable, the detail on that vase. On Penelope's loom is a long piece of work—you can tell by the amount of it completed and rolled up—and the piece she has been working on has a frieze of winged creatures, a griffin, a winged horse, a human figure with huge wings arching from his shoulders and tiny spur-wings on his heels, a little winged dog...."

She shook her head. "But it was on Cyprus, a couple of weeks after that, where I had the experience that changed my life."

"Hang on. You're moving too fast."

She still had her spectacles on, and now she pushed them down on her nose and peered over them. "I'll spare you how I got to Cyprus. The point is that at Paphos there are incredible Greek mosaics, and on the way to see them we passed the birthplace of Aphrodite. It's exactly the place where she rose from the waves in Botticelli's painting. The Venus on the shell. I studied that painting for ages later, in Florence. The dry brown fingers of land pointing out into the sea and then suddenly, the arrival of love in the world. He's made her so delicate, floating on scalloped waves, so expressionless, as if she's newly hatched without the faintest idea of the force she's about to let loose on the world. When you are there, on the spot, the place has a most peculiar, charged atmosphere...."

Allegra had been in Cyprus with a lover, Brad guessed. Or with her husband, Patrick. In either case a complication was close at hand. Behind all these stories, was the implicit presence of a man. Sometimes she forgot herself and took Brad into her confidence completely. Brad had begun to recognize the rhythm of Allegra's conversations, the way a door might open to send him into a world he'd never explored, and all at once he'd find himself in Cyprus or Florence or Morocco, carried by her words.

"So, then?"

"Oh well, so then," Allegra laughed. "So then we get to the point of this, at last. I was tramping along the road, along this high cliff above the sea, and I saw a little rocky side-road leading up the hill, with a sign indicating that it led to Aphrodite's shrine. In a few minutes, I came out on a high grassy plain with the ruins of the temple lying about: enormous fluted columns and the sea below. I began to get the most peculiar sensation standing there, a prickle on my skin, as if something very important was about to be revealed."

"I saw signs leading to a little museum, and eventually a caretaker came, took my money, let me in, then left me completely alone in a room full of wine jugs that Homer might have touched, or the heroes he wrote about. Things dating back five thousand years or more, out in the open where I could have touched them. And then in a far corner, I caught sight of the most remarkable Greek amphora. Most of them have battle scenes, or chariot races, or male athletes taking part in games; but all around this one, there was a frieze of women—women weaving, and spinning, and dying cloth—so beautiful and calm. They were wearing lovely clothes, graceful belted dresses with wide borders and patterns that looked like stars...preparing wool and folding cloth.... How rare that is. Half the population of the world, working from dawn until dusk. How many times is that recorded?"

She laughed. "That was all there was to it, really. At the shrine celebrating the very thing that had repeatedly got me into trouble, a shrine to love, I found myself so hopeful."

"That's when I left Patrick. Well, a lot of things contributed to that. I spent a couple of years travelling around Europe, working in weaving studios wherever I could, often just for my room and board. The more I learned, the more obsessed I became. I even went back to Africa—well Arabia—before I came home. By then I'd learned about the weaving the Bedouins did and I wanted to see for myself, the way they weave everything, even their tents, on enormous looms they lay out on the ground wherever they stop, looms that are merely sticks and poles propped up with rocks, and the warp stretching off into the desert some twenty feet or so, held tight by drag-weights. So basic," she said. "I felt I was learning the secret of something so essential. Imagine being able to lay out a few sticks on the ground to weave your house!"

"And that's how I got into this." She laughed. "The shorter version. Now come on," she led him toward the front room, "I'll pour you a glass of FibreWorks special vintage." She locked the shop door and put the "Closed" sign up. "Do you prefer yellow, red or blue?"

$\wp$

The apothecary jars poured a residue of colour on the hardwood floor. Brad, seated in a deep chair covered with a woven throw, holding a pottery mug of wine, did feel that there might be alchemy at work. Suddenly his thoughts seemed molten, he couldn't stop their flow. He found himself telling Allegra: how he had never dated a girl like Mona before, an art-school student, the daughter of a banker; how Mona had made an effort at first, when Brad had taken her to his mother's place on Commercial; how she sat in the living room with the sparkle-plastered ceiling, heavy plush-covered furniture, chocolate satin cushions with pink frills, all things that Brad himself, on that occasion, had seen with new eyes; how Brad's mother, in her good black funeral suit, her diamond-and-garnet broach, her lizard shoes, had been more than a match for a West Vancouver girl, serving walnut torte after the heavy dinner, coffee topped with whipped cream in thin, rose-patterned cups, overcoming Mona's sensibilities completely with sugary old world charm and several thousand calories.

He even told Allegra about Mona's letter. How she'd made a confession.

"Do you think she really might come back?"

"No."

"Just like that? 'No'?"

Allegra was looking at him closely.

"What kind of work is Mona doing these days?"

"Installations," he said. "Gender-based. In other words, I don't really know."

"But you don't like it."

"I didn't say that."

Last year, in Vancouver, Mona had put up an installation of female torsos, pink swollen pregnant shapes with bright red lips, wide open, avid as baby birds—the top of their heads cut off so you could see the emptiness inside.

"I saw her show here last year," Allegra was saying. "You've got to admit that was powerful."

"It almost cost her the funding to go to Toronto though."

"What?"

"You didn't see the review the critic from *The Globe* wrote? A diatribe about how her work objectified the female form?"

"Yes, I do remember that. But wasn't that written by a man?"

"So you discount it?" The wine made him reckless, confused.

"You're pretty touchy about this."

"I guess I've just spent too much time enduring Mona's politics."

He had learned something since she left. He knew that art did not require hours of discussion about power relations and gender and reclaiming certain types of work (female) as legitimate practice —you just picked up a pencil and you drew.

"Mona did get her funding, though? The collective didn't cut her off?"

"No, the women loved her work. Last time she called she said she was onto something new."

"What is it?"

He shrugged. "She's exploring the domination of the phallic form in clay."

They laughed. Colour flooded Allegra's face.

"So when do I see your work?" she asked.

"My work? You're seeing it all day."

"I mean the real work. Come on, I saw you at Opus. You were buying tubes of oils. Shall I tell you what you were buying? Black oxide and yellow ochre and cerulean blue."

As she registered his confusion, she reached out and touched his knee, her fingers weaving through the rip in his jeans.

§

The day after Brad had completed all Allegra's mirrored walls, he started work in the Properties. Several thousand dollars worth of tinted thermal windows had been broken during a home invasion.

Along the side of the house, the walkways crunched and sent up fragments of hot light. Brad finished taking the measurements and packed up his tools. He bought some wine, some olive bread, some grapes and camembert. He passed a florist. He bought a single bird-of-paradise.

Allegra had just stepped out of the shower. She came to the door wearing a white terrycloth robe.

Her hair was damp and heavy and sweet against his face, soaking the pillow and her flowered sheets.

August

When Procne, the daughter of King Pandion of Athens, married Tereus, the king of Thrace, the omens were not good. But Procne was beautiful and Tereus was rich, so no one paid attention as the Furies barged into the wedding procession, carrying funeral torches, to light the couple to their marriage bed. An owl perched on the roof and sometimes mewed and sometimes screamed, on that night when their son Itys was conceived.

Five years went by. Procne loved her husband, but she became lonely in far-off Thrace. At last she persuaded Tereus to sail to Athens, to beg her father to allow her sister to visit.

That is how the story of Philomela begins. This is a tale of voice, a tale of song. Above all a tale of the power of woven cloth.

Everywhere we turn in Greek myth, in stories that have worked their way into the very fabric of our language—of Philomela, of Arachne, of Niobe, of Penelope of course—there is lore of weaving running through. Can we trace it back to the Mycenaeans, those great warriors and organizers who trickled into the Greek peninsula at the start of recorded history? They built citadels upon the hilltops. Their bards sang stories of their exploits which filtered into myth. They invented a form of writing, on clay tablets, which we now describe as Linear B. But these first writings of the Greeks were nothing grand: only palace accounts, mainly to do with rations and supplies for their textile workers (women captured during Homeric raids) detailing who wove what, and what she ate (wheat and figs).

"The men were put to the sword, and the women sold into slavery." When we read histories of those times, that phrase leaps out again and again. The victors made it into the songs and poems. The rest disappeared. Of those captured women who went on to spin the cloth that became a principle source of Aegean wealth, we have the merest tally—except possibly for Agamemnon's mention of "The fair-cheeked Chryseis...walking up and down at the loom and tending my bed."

§

Allegra did not intend to keep her looms in storage for long. These days she thought of weaving more and more.

Outside her window, on the seawall, it was finally summer after weeks of rain. Evening sounds from the park by the water drifted up to her, the cries of children, the hiss of bike wheels and roller-blades, the music of an ice-cream vendor coming into earshot then moving away. On days when her strength ebbed and she did not have the energy to go out into the sun, Brad's mirrors brought in sailboats streaking across the bay, the freshness of the sea.

This evening Faye sat at Allegra's table cutting out a pattern of dogwood blooms, performing the delicate work that Allegra's hands could not manage anymore. Her elfin face puckered in concentration as she cut shapes for Allegra to arrange on brown waxed paper, then glued them down, cut out the dark spaces in between. Allegra held back from sharing all she burned with, her unexpected happiness and unexpected dread.

The first day he'd come over Brad hadn't remembered who she was. That had been a shock, because she recalled so well that day he had come into the shop. A dark young man—bulging forehead, splendid nose, brooding eyes—he had skulked while Mona looked around. He inspected the door handle, which was loose. He whipped a screwdriver from his hip pocket and took apart the whole mechanism of the double lock. When he realized she was watching, the handle swung loose, scattering screws on the floor. She went over and knelt with him to gather them up. Their hands touched. He smiled. Since that long-ago encounter, she had felt a flush of pleasure every time she'd seen him. He was out there all these years, as remote as the moon.

To have the moon slip in through your window was a different matter: in between your curtains, in between your sheets. That was something she had never expected once her illness had forced her to move to this apartment. Yet, if she hadn't moved, she would never have called him. A blessing in disguise?

"Do you know what a blessing is?" she asked Faye suddenly.

"I think you're going to tell me."

"It's the collective name for unicorns. A pride of lions, a skulk of foxes, a plague of locusts, a blessing of unicorns."

"You know you're in trouble when you go on about unicorns." Faye's sharp knife slid through the waxed paper, and the background fell away. "Careful. We don't want you pulling a Lady of Shalott."

Allegra laughed and tried to ignore the shadow that slid through the room. She turned to that blessing of unicorns, their white flanks dappled and obscure, their mild heads lowered as they grazed—invisible, except when the purple half-light spiralled from the toss of a pointed horn. A blessing. Something no one else can see.

No, certainly she would not sell her looms. The studio would soon produce beautiful woven goods to coordinate with the printed cloth. There would be feature articles in *Architectural Digest, Habitat, Better Homes and Gardens.* Even if she did not recover the strength to weave again, she would have the means to train full-time assistants. She would experiment with Ikat, the ancient technique in which individual threads are tied and dyed before the loom is warped, causing images to surface that are surprising, mysterious, hazy outlines that seem unrelated to the overall texture of the weave. The way things come up in life, Allegra thought; or the way they seemed to be emerging in her own secret tapestry, the one Brad had caught her working on recently. It had grown darker and darker over the last few years, had developed into a pattern of black rocks in an indigo stream, ominous when she stood back to see how the design was progressing. What she had intended was an abstract image, indicating stepping stones. Then almost without willing it, one day she had begun looping in the shades of a bright flower.

୨

Allegra was beginning to have trouble with the heat, even in this breezy room. "Do you think you could take the plant sprayer," she asked Faye, "and spritz my head?"

"As if you were a lily, like the one you are secretly weaving on that piece behind the cupboard door?"

"You recognized it as a lily?" She could feel herself begin to flush.

"Of course."

"I had a lot of trouble with that. It took me almost a week, just to work that one rough flower."

"I've never seen that loom before. I didn't know that you worked in tapestry as well." Faye enveloped Allegra in lovely cooling mist. "Grow," she said. "Grow, grow, grow!"

"Enough. You're drenching me."

"It's so encouraging you can do that. The technique is twining, isn't it?"

"In part. Twining and soumak. Here and there. When I first came home from Europe I was inspired by native weaving, Chilkat blankets in particular. I was so broke, and I was impressed by the remarkable designs they had been able to create with the simplest of looms—and no need for all that business of weaving from the back, only seeing what you were doing in a mirror...."

"This looks complex, though, the way the design moves, so many gradations of colour."

"If I use a large enough bobbin, I can manage. I haven't been able to wind the weft into a butterfly for a while. I get it all tangled in knots, but bobbins are fine, if I'm patient. And it's a project I've been working on for years. I make myself do a bit of it now and then, no matter how clumsy I've become. It's the story of my life."

"I'd love to see the whole of it."

Allegra laughed. "Me too."

"Let me look closer at you," Faye was saying. "Do you realize I can see the whole room mirrored upside down in the drops of water in your hair? What an amazing illusion. You're sparkling. I noticed the moment I came in; you looked suspiciously radiant today."

The urge to tell was terrible. To dwell on every detail of what had happened, when Brad had turned up unexpectedly as she stepped out of the shower.

℘

He pushed into her apartment carrying bread and wine and a tall exotic flower, and dropped them all on the floor. She felt that she'd just wakened from a drugged century of sleep, waiting for this man with his wide mouth to slide his hands across her stomach and down the inside of her thighs, never taking his eyes from her eyes, devouring her expression, pulling himself so deeply into both her body and her heart that she could feel herself bursting apart with the hope of this.

"I want to know everything about you," he said afterwards, his voice blurring the words, the way a person might say something quickly into the mouth of the phone, knowing someone was listening.

"Is that why you kept your eyes open?" she said, as she traced the architecture of his ribs.

He twisted himself up cross-legged on the bed. His dark eyes crinkled at the corners like a disconsolate child's. She saw what she always saw too late—how making love was the first step away, the first step toward misunderstanding—how the last chance had slipped past, when you weren't looking.

"Come on. Nobody ever really knows anybody else," she said. "You get fragments, bits that pierce the mist, and then you make assumptions about the rest. For example, I see this." She pulled him down so she could kiss his nose. "And this." His penis, curled up again, shy as a snail. "And I make the assumption that there is a heart somewhere in between."

<p>

"Did you know that the unicorn appears in stories from all over the world?" she said to Faye. "From India to the Near East to Greece?"

"Really?"

"Such a persistent creature could hardly be a myth, could it? Traditionally, they are invisible to all but virgins, which makes them hard to track. The hunt for the unicorn was a major preoccupation in Medieval times. For one thing, the horn is an antidote to poison. Also, knife handles made out of it turn black if the knife touches poisoned food, and the handle gives off little beads of liquid. That was important to know, in the olden days, because poison was a common remedy for all sorts of inconveniences and ills."

"How did you come to know all this?"

"I must have read it somewhere. The Hunt for the Unicorn was a favorite subject of medieval *wedding* tapestries too..."

"Okay, what's going on?" Faye said. "What is all of this about?"

She reached across and took from Allegra's hands the wobbling square of paper that held the next design.

The sun pressed on the mountains across the strait; a sweet orange light poured from the mirror on the balcony, spreading through the room.

"It was so easy at first," Allegra found herself saying. "I didn't worry if he called, or if he didn't. I had so much damn power.

Amazing, isn't it? Dragging around like this, and feeling all lit up with power."

"But now you care."

She nodded. "And it is so ridiculous. It's delusion. What does he need a sick person my age for?"

"He's the lucky one. We are talking about Brad, I assume."

"Then why..." Allegra felt embarrassed now. Her worry kept to herself had swelled and swelled. "Why is he so secretive? He has never once asked me to his house. Every time I suggest it, he changes the subject."

"I expect he doesn't want to clean it. Careful. You're going to break that chain!"

"Why hasn't he let me meet his little boy?" Allegra realized that she had been pulling at the spidery chain of her gold locket.

"That locket is so beautiful. I love antique gold. Tell me where it came from."

She saw Brad's dark, liquid eyes and remembered how it felt to have someone say they wanted to know all about you, say "tell me".

She had never told the story of her locket to anyone.

If she gave him all her secrets, wasn't it just possible that everything might change: her body heal: fish pull themselves flopping from the sea to learn to fly?

The sun slid down, lighting up the row of cures and potions on the counter near the sink, the aloe-vera caplets, and the blue-green algae, and an amber vial of evening primrose oil. In this light she could believe anything. The spider plant was gilded, in the corner where it breathed poisons from the air.

Just as Tereus was explaining to King Pandion why it was he had unexpectedly appeared in Athens, how Procne longed to see her sister, he stopped, mid-word. Philomela had entered the room, richly dressed, yet unaware that her own loveliness was the most dazzling of her adornments. At that moment, Ovid tells us, "Tereus felt his blood alter thickly," as desire flamed in him. He told himself her beauty was to blame. Even as he stood there, half in tears, persuading Philomela's father how desperately Procne needed to see her sister, it was his own sick lust that made his tale so convincing. Everyone who heard was deeply touched by how he pleaded for the happiness of his wife. "God in heaven, how blind men are!" Ovid says.

After a royal banquet Tereus lay awake all night, feeding his desire with images of Philomela's beauty and her graces and all he intended to possess.

§

A breeze rustled around the terrace of the restaurant in Stanley Park. Allegra looked out at the last of the golden evening sliding down the leaves of the great maples growing on the grass. She could see across to the lawn-bowling court, where white-clad figures moved in the slow rhythms of their final game before it became too dark. She was nervous. She decided to ease into this conversation with the sort of story that Brad seemed to love. Lately, when she hesitated or held back, she felt silence oozing out of him like something sore.

"You know, there was a day when I really thought I might learn to fly." She lifted her arms and spread them. She was wearing a voile dress so faded that the paisley fluttered like soft petalled wings. "I was a teenager. In the Okanagan. I used to run down to the lake and along the shore. One day I ran all the way out of town and up a hill in the middle of the orchards. When I was little my dad told me it had once been a volcano, though I think that was because after my mother left he took a cataclysmic view of things. His family used to own all the acreage at the base of the hill, but he lost it; when she left he went to pieces for a while.

"When I got to the top of the mountain, I stood with my arms stretched, looking up the valley at the sweep of lake far below, the water brushed by wind into patterns, the same wind rushing in my face, pulling at my blouse—anything was possible. Two weeks later I got pregnant," she said. "In that very same spot, more or less. Graduation night.

"So that explains my lack of a college education," she said into the silence. "I let them take her for adoption," she added. She thought she'd caught Brad glancing nervously around the terrace, as if her child might suddenly appear. "I gave this to her." She fingered the gold locket. "It was my mother's too; she left it in an envelope for me, when she ran away. I put my picture in it along with hers, and just before I had to give her up I pinned it to her clothes. But the social worker sent it back."

She could not read Brad's expression.

"So I have a daughter, and I've never seen her," she concluded. "Not since she was five days old. I don't even know her name. No, that's not true. Her name is Angeline. No matter what someone else has called her."

"You could try to find her. There are agencies that do that, aren't there?"

"Oh, I have tried. I'm starting to think she doesn't want to be found. I just need to know that she's okay," Allegra said. "Even though I don't know how I'd ever explain...."

"She'd understand. She understands that already, Allegra. She's your daughter isn't she?"

It was like talking in the dark, the dusky closeness she felt now. He was beautiful, his hair grown long these last weeks, flying out in disobedient waves he ran his fingers through. Now he leaned toward her, his hands gripping the sides of the table as if he were clinging to the prow of a ship. She let the intimate silence wash around them, prepared to give him all her remaining gifts.

As they resumed the meal, she showed him how you ate mussels in a Paris bistro or on the beach in Portugal—how you used one jointed shell like a pair of tongs, to pluck the meat. He had never been to Paris. She described a lunch she'd had once, at least a dozen different types of shellfish that had been opened by a stout white-aproned man out on the street just minutes before, oysters, clams, scallops, winkles, other creatures holding on inside of turban shells. She told him about other meals from other travels, *plükfisk, bouillabaise* and *kelftiko*. Little by little, she added detail, like adding sticks of kindling to a fire.

"I have a high school secret, too," he said.

§

Miss Carson did not look like a high-school teacher. Her hair hung halfway down her back in a fat plait, as thick as a braided loaf Brad's Norwegian grandmother used to make. She wore denim skirts, blouses that had been embroidered in Mexico or Guatemala, with strings that laced through the V-neck. She took to keeping Brad after school to coach him for his history exams. She knew he was smart, yet he had flunked his test about the re-alignment of

European nations after the Second World War.

"Let me put it this way, Brad...."

He described the indrawn breath that pulled the cross-stitch at the front of her cotton blouse tight across her chest, before she leaned forward with her elbows on the desk and made a tent of her hands around her nose. She had long brown hands, but she bit the nails down to the quick. "I felt somehow responsible for making her job easier, so I smiled."

Allegra could see that: Miss Carson tapping her two index fingers on her nose, how the steeple of her hands would slide down to her chin, when Brad smiled.

"Let's put it this way," Miss Carson had said. "Lindhall. What sort of name is that? What country of origin, I mean?"

"My dad was born in New Westminster."

"But your grandparents? Lindhall strikes me as Scandinavian, right?"

Brad shrugged.

"Come on, give me some help. This is Vancouver. Everybody comes from somewhere else. And what I want to explore is how that happened—how that relates to this exam...."

But Brad had not wanted to learn about the fluctuating map of Europe or what had happened to bring his mother here.

"Why not?" Allegra asked.

It was alarming, the flat black look that eclipsed his features. Instead of answering, he told her about how he started seeing Miss Carson after that. Seeing her. During afternoons when he was supposed to be at basketball practice, until the end of the term, when Miss Carson moved away.

"Did anybody know?"

Brad shook his head.

"She could be sent to jail now, you know." Allegra tried to take his hand, but he pulled back.

"That's ridiculous. It was worse for her than for me."

※

She would show him her tapestry tonight, reveal to him how it was meant for Angeline, how with bumbling loops of weft, and later with growing skill, she had begun unrolling the events of her whole life: not in pictures but in symbols, abstract patterns, arrangements of colour. The lotus bloom that cracked into two halves of a heart: Allegra had worked that motif over and over in varying shades, later winding it into a long and flowing frieze that took on the aspects of a vine. Perhaps her daughter would see Allegra clearly enough to tell her what this whole tapestry meant. A child can *see* a mother, really see her. A mother can come into focus for herself in the eyes of a child. Allegra would explain all that to Brad, how she would always feel she had lost the most important aspect of herself until she found her child. Then Brad would see how, under her vagrant hands, despite her illness, the pattern had begun to veer and the colours darken, revealing moods that even she hardly recognized.

Brad had come in one day not long after he started work on the mirrors and surprised her just as she was working a lily into that somber field. This is you, she would say to him tonight. In the mess of my life, this lovely thing.

"I better not come up," Brad said when he had driven her home and seen her to the elevator.

"Why not? I want you to see something."

"I'll come over on Friday. Or...whenever. Mrs. Chan is having trouble with her father-in-law. I'll have to see what I can arrange. I'll give you a call."

"You'll give me a call."

"Okay?" He nuzzled behind her ear.

"No, not okay. I've started to get used to having you around. If the sitter is the problem, why don't I come over to your place?" Though her car had packed it in, she could take a bus. He didn't have to feel responsible for driving her. A bus, and a taxi home.

"Look. I'm on this job out in the valley. I have to get up at five every day this week and drive Nicky over to the sitter's to get to work on time. Let's leave it until the weekend."

"I meant the weekend. We could take Nicky to the beach. We've known each other all this time and I've never met your child!"

A fat moon had risen over the apartment tower next door. It poured into the courtyard where they stood, every bush and leaf silver and crisp.

"I'll call."

He pushed her code. The door opened. The glass cube carried her away.

September

"*I lend my daughter to you,*" *Pandion said as the ship of Tereus set sail. "By your honour, by the gods, protect her like a father." The painted ship slipped from the land. Tereus laughed; Philomela could feel his eyes on the nape of her neck.*

The moment the ship arrived on his own shore, Tereus lifted the girl onto a horse and carried her off to a high tower hidden in the forest. She looked around with growing fear, asking to see her sister. His only answer was to tear off her clothes.

Afterwards she crouched shuddering in a corner, "like a woman in mourning," filled with horror and with shame; how could she ever face her sister now? She gouged her arms with her fingernails, clawed her hair, and began to shriek at Tereus, shaming him for breaking his oath to her father, and to his wife.

§

The early days of September were mellow, golden, the sun like honey, soothing fevered moments.

Work did this too. Orders for the placemats were flooding in. The production had to be arranged and overseen. The sewing was done as piece-work, by women with small children who were glad to have work to do at home.

"At sweat shop rates I bet," Brad said. When Allegra tried to talk to him about business, he became forbearing, disapproving. Recently everything to do with the business, the tension, the aggravation, but particularly the excitement, seemed to turn him into a resolute protector. The work took too much out of her, he said.

"I don't know why everything is about love and romance," she said to Faye, on the phone one afternoon. "We spend half our lives working, the rest of it asleep. Love is just that little mosquito that buzzes around and disturbs our dreams."

"Allegra, this pessimism is unlike you."

"Just feel the need to get out, I guess. Are you sure you don't need me to come down, this afternoon?"

She was on a path by the sea in English Bay. A few days ago she had taken possession of a new motorized chair. Brad had arranged it for her and had given her a cell phone for her birthday.

The less she saw of him—he was still tied up with a big job out in Chilliwack—the more he did for her. He had done all the paperwork about the chair, taken care of all the forms the department of health required.

56

"No, go and enjoy yourself," Faye said. "Manny and Jim have almost got the padding on the table, and I'm shooting the photo screens so we can work up the huckleberry print. The first one was ruined. I must have over-shot it. I had a lot of trouble getting the coating out of all those fine lines and tiny leaves."

"That new emulsion is so finicky. But we'll need it when we start making really durable screens for long runs." Last week they had ruined three of their small test screens by over-exposing. Jim had needed to strip the mesh off and re-stretch them.

"I'm going to take some pictures of sambuca while I'm down here," Allegra said. "There's a bush of it up in the park."

She rested the phone on her lap and maneuvered the wheel chair into the shade of a spreading maple across from the concession stand, then wedged the phone into the crook between her shoulder and her chin.

"I want to get some shots of the berries against the sky, and if they work out we can use the negative directly on the screens. Did Brad call me there, by the way? I realized I had the phone turned off for a while. He was going to call and let me know about arrangements for the weekend."

"What's happening on the weekend?"

"If the weather holds, some friends of his family have a cabin on Mayne Island, and he's arranged for us to stay. It was one of my presents. I'd been thinking he'd forgotten my birthday altogether, and then he turned up after work and whisked me over to that Cuban restaurant on Commercial and sprang this surprise and gave me a silver necklace. A choker. A bit too tight, but he said he'd fix it. Silver and lapis, beautiful."

The stones were set in rounds of scalloped silver joined by

delicate chains of filigree. She would have loved it, a few years ago. Even if he managed to enlarge it, it would feel too heavy and constraining. Anyway, Brad knew she never took off her locket.

"Is Nicky coming with you on the weekend?" Faye asked.

"No, Brad has managed to get Mrs. Chan for the entire time! Cross your fingers this doesn't fall through. She's had a lot of family trouble, lately, and she's one of those dutiful daughters, I take it; whenever something comes up she puts her family first. Of course I've never met her. You'd think Brad had a body buried in the basement, wouldn't you? The efforts he goes to, to keep me out of his home life."

Curiosity, she thought. That's what urges us forward as we creep from room to room in another person's mind, prying open the doors of secret chambers, desperate to learn what produces this love that overcomes us.

♇

Maybe all history was excavation, subject to the same interpretative acts as archaeology. Fragments. What you didn't know you could invent. She and Brad had settled at a table at Cárdenas on the night of her birthday. Cuban music in the background gave her the fine sensation of escape.

It was the day of her birth, yet what of *his*, of his childhood? She knew that his father had died when he was a child. Lindhall. But the family was not Scandinavian; his mother was Romanian. She died just before Nicky was born.

"Actually, she didn't know that we were going to have a baby," Brad told Allegra once. "She really wanted a grandchild. She would have been so pleased."

His mother kept nagging Brad to get Mona to settle down and have a child. She didn't understand what Mona did, why Brad couldn't get her to change. She thought that being an artist was painting icons, and she had even offered to introduce Mona to two sisters she knew in North Vancouver who painted icons on glass, which would make Mona a bit of spending money, she said. When Mona refused, his mother didn't speak to Brad for a month.

He had been at the beck and call of his mother. One day he drove Allegra past the house where he'd grown up, near the Skytrain off Commercial, a square stucco house with a plate glass window and red cement steps. His mother had worked in a fish plant for years. Brad had the whole east end to roam in when he was a kid, left to the care of his invalid father, at home. Allegra formed a picture of his mother: a haunting face with eyes like Brad's, eyes that tilted into huge dark teardrops, a fringe of bobbed black hair, covered with a red print scarf, rubber gloves to protect her white hands and painted nails.

"Do you still have family in Romania?" she asked now. She toyed with her re-fried beans and noticed how Brad's face closed abruptly, a visor snapping shut. "That was where she was from?"

He shrugged, his face suddenly blank.

She told him about *her* father, who had briefly been mayor of the town where she grew up, "though by the time I went back to live with him after a brief spell at my aunt's, he had lost everything; he was working in the ticket office of the bus station, and we lived in a little house by the creek. My mother ran off with a cowboy, when I was four. Did I tell you that? It was a pretty big scandal, as you can imagine, in our little farming community."

"Your father took it hard."

"It's a long story. How many times have I said that?"

"I just like the way you look, when you say it. The way you crinkle up your forehead."

"It's a story Brad. Not a performance. My dad owned a big orchard and when my mother left he threw everything away —though I later realized he was already terribly in debt. I think he was probably drinking a lot in those days, even before she left. She was so pretty, so much fun. She used to put polish on my nails. When she left, the thing I couldn't get over was that they didn't take me with them. I actually met him for a few minutes, you know—the cowboy, Slim Jordan. *I* fell in love with him, too."

She was conscious of Brad's dark eyes pulling this out of her, and of what a fine thing it was once you got started, to be able to unreel your life in conversation.

"I was out with my aunt, one day," she carried on. "My father's sister. That's important. We were shopping, and then she realized she'd left her purse at our place, and had to go back. When we got there, we found an enormous white car in the drive, with fins. I could tell my aunt was furious, though I didn't understand why. I'd never seen a car like it. Aunt Liz got out and strode into the house, telling me to stay right where I was. By the time I got inside she and my mom were having a fierce whispering fight, in the bedroom, and a tall, thin man was leaning against the kitchen sink, drinking a bottle of beer. I thought he was a movie star. He had a huge silver buckle on his belt, in the shape of a steer's head. When he saw me looking at his belt buckle he called me over and told me how he'd won it riding in the rodeos. He rode Brahma bulls.

"I asked him if it was dangerous, and he said, 'Not if I've got the right lady looking on.' At that moment my mother came out of the bedroom, and they exchanged smiles, and my aunt slammed out the door. Next morning when I got up, my mom was gone. She used to send me postcards, pretending she was off on a holiday. When I was seven she died in a car crash."

"That's grim," Brad said.

"And I know practically nothing about my mother's family, you know. She came from overseas. I always meant to get all that information, but it was hard to talk to Dad about it; and now that he has died too, I'll never know."

The server brought their paella. A pretty woman with a bristle of hair. She was wearing a long white shirt and lycra biking shorts, speeding between the tables with the tray held high above her head, sweeping down oval platters in front of them, loaded with rice, chicken, chorizo and prawns.

"I've always wanted to make this," Allegra said. I love Spanish food. Did your mother cook Romanian dishes? I had something called *giveche* once. *Giveche cu carne*? It was rather like this, only rice and lamb...."

"They forgot the hot sauce." Brad said craning around to attract the attention of the server.

"Would you like to go?" she pressed on. "Now that it's easier to get a visa.... I've read about their painted monasteries; they're supposed to be world treasures. But that's all I really know. Just Dracula and Ceausescu," she said. "That's awful isn't it, to be so ignorant. I knew a guy at school though, whose parents were refugees from Romania, during the war. He told me about a fascist cult that almost took over the country."

"Hang on," Brad said. "Excuse me."

He got up and headed toward the back, through the gallery, to the washrooms. When he returned, she kept her questions to the matter of the cabin on Mayne Island.

"What's the place like?"

"Just a cabin. I haven't been there for ages. You'll see."

"Who owns it, though?"

"I told you. Some distant cousins of my dad's."

℘

By the pool at Second Beach, Allegra got a diet coke. She drank it at the concession stand, to prevent it from spilling on her lap, then fished out the ice cubes and dropped them inside the back of her shirt. She could feel the onset of fatigue. She maneuvered the chair to a shady place where she could look down on a curve of beach. Children dashed into the water screaming, laughing. People streamed past, everyone on the move.

She watched a couple setting up beach chairs in the sun. The woman stood with her hands jammed into the pockets of her cargo pants, supervising as the man arranged the chairs and hamper and umbrella and newspapers and magazines. Three times she changed her mind, squeaking, "No ROGER, not THERE," and he laughed a hearty desperate laugh as he took down the umbrella, folded the chairs and moved the whole assembly until she finally consented. Perhaps the woman's unpredictable moods gave Roger something real to hold onto, something he needed. Had Mona provided that for Brad? A toughness that Allegra was no longer well enough to match? Was there a dragon of despair in Brad that cried out to be kicked?

Her hand accidentally flicked the controls. Her chair swivelled. She was not used to this machine yet. She slammed into someone coming along the path—a quick impression of a styrofoam cup, a spill of liquid directed away onto the ground.

"Oh, I'm so sorry...."

A man in his fifties, bulky, but athletic, agile. He leapt out of the way and then turned with a look of expectation, as if this had been the first measure of an old-fashioned dance he'd slightly fumbled. "Are you all right?" he asked with concern.

She was staring at him. He was dressed in a creamy linen jacket and fine linen pants. He wore leather loafers and wine-coloured socks. The coffee had spilled not just on the pavement, but also on his clothes.

"I'm so sorry about your pants. I should have looked where I was going."

"It was my fault absolutely." He had an accent that she couldn't place, eastern European perhaps. His short beard reminded her of someone. His silvery hair coiled in tight curls. He bowed almost as if he might reach to kiss her hand. His eyes held a glint of silver too, and then a glint of gold, like water over sand.

"No doubt it serves me right for coming down here when I ought to be at work," he said. She liked the growl of his voice, the jumble of his words.

"I was feeling guilty about that, myself. But are you sure you're okay? I haven't had this chair long, I'm still a bit out-of-control."

"It is a beautiful machine." He sounded genuinely admiring, as if she were at the wheel of a new car.

He squatted to examine the gear mechanism, flicking the lever so she rolled a bit this way and that. The top of his head was level with her knee. His hand on the control stick was very tanned. On the middle finger was a wide gold ring with a band of leaves.

His inspection of her chair led her to ask about his work, though later she realized she had not gotten all the facts. He was an occupational therapist, or managed a clinic, or perhaps owned one.

"I have travelled all around the world," he said. "But now I settle here." He had a good understanding of the problems she faced in getting around, also of the hoops one had to jump through in order to be assigned such a chair. They fell into conversation naturally as they continued along the seawall. She had to be careful to adjust her pace to his, but managed to stay parallel in the walking lane.

She did not see the fallen alder branch until it was too late. It must have cracked in last night's wind. It was hanging over the path just at the height of her head. They had been counting the freighters at anchor, looking out to sea. One of the broken twigs scraped her face, and another her neck, catching hold of her locket. She crashed through the mesh of twigs and leaves, not managing to stop the chair for twenty feet.

"Oh no. Oh no!" She clutched at her neck, feeling for the chain. "It's caught on that branch somewhere. Can you see it?"

When she turned back, she saw him searching through the leaves. Such a fine thing, such a small thing. Though it would gleam. But what if a crow caught that gleam and swooped down and grabbed it away? What if it had fallen down that storm grate?

"I have it!" he called.

"Is the chain broken?"

"Let me see. No it is completely fine. The clasp is perfect. It must just have twisted open."

"Are you sure it's safe to wear again?"

He fished out some glasses from his pocket and peered at the tiny clasp. "Yes, it's quite all right. What a delicate chain!"

He understood without asking, how her hands could not perform the simple task of doing it up. He came around behind her and shifted the weight of her hair and she could feel his heavy fingers working carefully at the nape of her neck. She could smell soap and a hint of wine and the rich complicated breath of a man who smokes cigars.

They stopped at a bench by Siwash Rock. Waves swished around the base of that black jagged cone; the water was a deep green that day. Siwash rock. A princess turned to stone. A cormorant had perched on the tree that grew on top of it.

Allegra found herself telling him about her childhood in the Okanagan. His silvery eyes drew this out of her. He was so compelling, yet had no stake in what she did or didn't say. She began to tell him about that night....

℘

A very dark night. No moon. On the mountain top a dozen cars were already parked, most of them belonging to boys from the basketball team.

Her date was nervous. They snuggled, but nothing happened. Neither of them smoked. His dad's car didn't even have a radio. He became silent when she asked to leave for the after-grad party at the beach. Then he grabbed her and gave her a long dry kiss.

By this time they'd been up there more than half an hour.

Suddenly cars started honking their horns, first one and then another; they'd honk and then drive off. Her date pushed her away and turned on the motor and started honking too.

Honk, if you've scored.

"He was all set to drive away, but I grabbed the keys right out of the ignition, I was so furious. And then.... Well, I won't go into the details."

Her new companion raised an eyebrow. She saw how details were the currency of trust.

"I was bigger than he was," Allegra said. "And furious that he'd used me that way. I told him that if he didn't do it, now that he'd smeared my reputation—it was very important to hang onto your reputation in those days—I would tell the whole school what a coward he was. It turned out not to be so very difficult, actually. He even kept trying to see me after that. I think he forgot that it had been meant as retribution. I was the one who got punished, of course. My aunt saw to it that I went to a home in Kamloops, where I lived till my daughter was born."

"Do you ever see this boy?"

"No." Strange, she realized, that Brad had not asked her this.

She told him about her tapestry, how every day she tried to add a row of colour to some part of the design. "I *have* to see Angeline again."

He was looking somber, thoughtful. His forehead furrowed, his eyebrows tilting up like wings.

"Maybe I can help you," he said. "I don't want you to get up your hopes. But..."

He knew people. He could pull strings. He came from a

background where the rules were often bent, sometimes for the common good. None of that needed to be explained.

He came from an island in the Aegean, originally, he said. "You will not have heard of it. Very small." He left when he was just a child, raised by his father who was (perhaps) a shipping magnate. A powerful man, the father, at any rate.

"My mother died in an explosion, but I survived and grew up with him in Italy." Since then he had travelled widely, he told her again, "Sometimes happy, sometimes sad."

A pleasant glow of insubstantiality had come over her. She was studying the pattern on his tie. Even on this hot day, a tie, though he had a less formal manner. The tie was creamy green with interlocking squares of deep maroon. A pattern of vines rambled through the squares. And behind him as they sat and talked was a slope where each leaf gleamed beneath a sun now well into the west. Allegra was amazed at the richness of the scene; and this only one scene among many, one atom of shape and colour on this golden afternoon.

"I am DiSemele," he said before he left her. "Here, I will give you my card." It was very plain, on thick stock, the heavily embossed wine letters stating simply, George DiSemele.

℘

The evening was humming with the extended breath of summer as she rode home, the sky blazing lemon at its farthest edge, one star above hanging in a basin of deep blue. She stopped above the beach to take this in.

A Frisbee whistled by her ear and landed skimming on the sand. She must have dozed off. A dream. She had been walking behind Brad down a long corridor, carrying a rifle. She took aim to shoot him in the back. This seemed a perfectly reasonable thing to do, but someone else must have taken a shot first. He made a popping sound like a balloon, and disappeared.

ᘐ

"Why didn't you kill me first?" Philomela said. "Then at least my ghost would have been innocent." On and on she went, calling on the gods to see what Tereus had done, telling him that even if he kept her locked up in that tower forever she would find a way to tell what he had done, for she still had her voice: every leaf in the forest would be her tongue, every rock a witness.

Tereus was amazed. He had not thought through the consequences of his deed. When she would not stop screaming he grabbed her by the hair and drew his sword.

Philomela closed her eyes, and offered her throat to the blade, still calling to her father and to the gods, cursing Tereus. He caught her tongue with bronze pincers, sliced it off. "The stump recoiled, silenced, into the back of her throat. But the tongue squirmed in the dust, babbling on"——shaping soundless words. It writhed like a snake's tail, "striving to reach her feet in its death-struggle." And the king, obsessed, dazed, returned to Philomela's mutilated body and raped her again and again.

Then he went home, burying the secret deep within. He told Procne that her sister had died on the journey. Procne took off her royal garments and dressed in black, and went into deepest mourning for a year.

ᘐ

The cabin on Mayne Island sat on a bluff. Two gnarled trees framed a view of water, further islands, the mountains of the mainland. The air smelled of sea-wrack, sunny rocks and pine. They arrived late in the afternoon, and though Allegra was exhausted from the journey—it was the furthest she had travelled in at least two years—as she sat on the porch in the silence, in the clear air, she felt in a daze of happiness.

"You know, I was worried about this, all knotted up with tension for the last two days," she confessed to Brad. "Now I can't even remember why."

Brad had made gin-and-tonics in tall, blue Scandinavian glasses. Everything in the kitchen cupboards was blue or green, the plates and bowls, the ample glassware. The rooms were furnished in white pine. There were braided rugs on the floor, knitted throws over the chesterfields and chairs, patchwork quilts on the beds. The log walls of the cabin gleamed with varnish.

Ice clinked in her glass. She breathed in the fine medicinal smell of quinine and gin. Brad, in a red flannel shirt and his old torn jeans, lay back in a cape cod chair next to her, his dark hair frizzy from the exertions of the day.

"Suppose," she said, "I was one of those people who ran everyday, always in the same direction. And suppose you did the same, just ahead of me, just around the next bend. We would never meet, unless one of us changed direction, reversed the order of things."

He had spent the whole day folding and unfolding her wheelchair, helping her in and out of it, pushing her onto the deck so she could enjoy the view of Active Pass, wheeling her through the crowded ship onto the elevator, back into the van again.

He didn't pay any attention to what she was saying. Just as well. Probably tonight—after they'd eaten the soup she'd brought in the cooler, and the cheese and apples and bread—he would fall asleep beside her in that white bed, beneath the quilt's double-wedding-ring design.

℘

There was a half-moon bay below the cabin. The path was steep and narrow, but the next morning Brad piggy-backed Allegra down, made her a tent of towels hung over driftwood roots so the heat wouldn't get to her, then went back for the picnic.

A peaceful, rustling wind mixed with the smell of the sand. Allegra's thoughts melted into the past, slipped away on the murmur of the sea. The towels flapped in the fresh-smelling breeze, and waves lifted pebbles along the shore, lifted them and let them fall, so that the sound touched every part of her body. She felt herself turn to a rock, the sun beating down, barnacles, mosses, lichens growing upon her, salal sprouting from her limbs.

"Maybe we could get a little place of our own over here," she heard herself say.

Brad was lying flat out on a log, naked, his hands hanging over the sides, his body a line of willful pieces that never quite relaxed, even asleep, even here. How helpless she was in this dazed and happy state, her puffed and suspect heart slit open by a lance of joy.

℘

She had told Brad how once she might have swum out to a small island that lay across the bay. "I swam right across Okanagan Lake when I was in highschool—from Trout Creek Point to Naramata. Sometimes I'm afraid I'll never do anything so spontaneous. I would love to be able to get out on the water sometime, get into a small boat, or a canoe, and set off and explore."

"Tilt your head," he said. "Like that, when you said spontaneous."

On that island, trees rimmed the sand, giving the place a wild, deserted look. In her thoughts, she had already started swimming away from him, remembering the freedom of a time when she could go anywhere she wanted, when she could wallow in loneliness and always make it back.

Brad broke the silence by telling her how that whole island had belonged to a rich eccentric.

"When I came here as a kid, he owned a private menagerie over there. All day long my cousin Lars and I could hear mysterious shrieks and brays of exotic animals. So one night we hiked over to the marina around the point, and helped ourselves to a boat. We spluttered across. There was a full moon. When we landed, we crept up through the trees. Finally we came upon a cluster of locked-up wooden pens. We could hear something moving around inside, but we couldn't see a thing. Then we heard this goddawful shriek. We were surrounded by peacocks, sleeping in the trees."

"Peacocks. No griffins or dinosaurs? What did you do then?"

"Without even discussing it we picked up rocks and started winging them at those birds. It was surreal."

"You killed them? The most beautiful birds in the world?"

He'd shrugged. "I don't know."

§

A crow flew over the makeshift tent of towels by the shore. She felt the shadow scraping overhead, and then the bird landed on a rock the tide had bared and started pecking mussel shells.

She looked over at Brad's long body lying naked on the log. "Brad," she called softly, "I need you. Please."

He came into her small tent, sun-dazed. Maybe she looked beautiful in that soft filtered light. Maybe it was this, as well as her need, that passed the need along. Enclosed in this small space, the sun dazzling outside, maybe the smell of her skin held an echo of all such hidden primal acts, hot flesh joining quickly in the shade.

His tongue was moving down her stomach, down through her pubic hair. She took his face between her hands. He raised himself before her at her touch. She licked every grain of sand from his upright penis. He would enter her and he would keep up the fiction that all of this had come from him. But she was crying, she couldn't help it. After his breath changed, became harsh, she delayed opening her eyes.

§

She watched the sand run through her fingers, its sharp and gleaming particles. She studied a heron on the shore. The lengthening shadows held a distillation of the day's heat. The waves lapped softly on the shore. The sun laid a golden slick on all the leaves.

Paradise. And in a moment she was going to spoil it. All at once this was clear. Nothing would help her, nothing could stop her. Look at the hunch of Brad's back as he pretended to read! She was going to struggle up, throw off the careful cover he'd arranged.

"All right, so we will never look for a little place over here, but at least you can let me see how you live. In three months, you have never let me in your house. You can't get out of the most basic commitment just by putting up mirrors, building shelves..."

She said a great deal more than that. Brad turned to her, his face so startled, stripped, scared, that words she'd never thought she might have in her exploded like grenades:

"WHY have you never let me visit you? WHY have you never let me meet your child? After all I've told you about my own loss, you must know how important that might be to me? WHY do you say you want to know all about me, when you don't listen, don't see? I can meet any man on the street and within five minutes he will have had the sensitivity to uncover more about me than you have in three months! NO WONDER your wife left you, if you only ever listen to what you want to hear!"

§

Now she was back at the cabin, lying exhausted on the bed, drained by weeping and all the outrageous things she had found to say. Terrible, such rage, and all of it really aimed at herself, her own condition.

She didn't know where Brad was. Perhaps he had gone for good, left her there. That might be better than facing a night in the same house and a long silent trip home. Evening was sifting down. The colours were starting to fade. She found herself wondering if you could capture the exact moment, if you were fleet, when the colours started to go?

§

She heard a van door slam. Brad's footsteps approached, entered the house, entered her room. She kept her eyes closed. He came and stood by the bed. He bent and picked her up, her sprawling arms and legs. He didn't say a word. He carried her out of the cabin, out to the car. They drove down a winding road, the headlights bobbing wildly, catching the huge splayed hands of maple leaves.

He carried her out onto a floating dock. A canoe was bumpered to the side. He strapped her into a life jacket, lifted her in, untied the boat and stepped in too. She didn't ask how he got the boat, or where he was taking her.

The canoe slipped softly through the water. The water whispered, grey as silk, everything gentle, unreal. The moon rose. A bird called.

§

Philomela, helpless, voiceless, at last saw what she could do. After months of captivity she gestured to her servants to set up a Thracian loom and on it, in detail, secretly she wove the story of what Tereus had done to her. When it was finished she wrapped the cloth and signalled to the most trusted of her servants to take this as a gift to the queen.

Procne unrolled the tapestry and understood its meaning immediately. She was staring at the ruination of her life. One single idea filled her head.

September

When the festival of Bacchus was upon them, Procne dressed as a Bacchante and joined the crowd of women that ran recklessly through the darkness, until she found the hidden tower in the forest. There, with howls to the god, the crowd of women tore down the gate. Procne freed her sister, disguised her as a reveler, brought her home and hid her safely in her room. But when she attempted to embrace her, Philomela, tortured with shame, wept and fixed her eyes on the ground. Procne shook her by the shoulders. "Tears cannot help us, only the sword...or something more pitiless even than the sword." She began to conjure up pictures of revenge: the palace in flames, Tereus blazing in it like an insect; hanging him by his tongue, sawing through it with a broken knife; digging his eyes out, butchering him.

Her little son Itys came in. He was a small reflection of his father. Her heart froze.

He came running to her, chattering, begging to be kissed. Her fury fell to a whisper. Tears burned her eyes. Then she caught him by the arm. She dragged him into a far cellar of the palace. She slashed his throat. The sisters tore apart his small hot body, the room red with blood. They cooked his remains, "some of it gasping in bronze pots, some weeping on spits." She invited her husband to a feast, saying this was a ritual of Athens, a feast day when the wife alone would serve her lord. Tereus was so happy, lolling on his throne, and the meal so delicious, that he wanted to share it with his son. "Where is Itys? Bring him!" he commanded.

Procne said, "He is here. He could not be nearer to you."

At that moment Philomela burst into the room, her hair and clothes all soaked in blood. She thrust into the face of Tereus the dismembered head of his son.

Tereus staggered, roared, sobbed—tore at his chest to rid himself of that meal. Bellowing murder he made chase down the long palace halls. But now all three of them were flying. A crest of feathers like the plume of a war *helmet had appeared on Tereus's head. Instead of a sword, he had the long curved beak of the hoopoe. Procne swooped, lamenting, round and round the palace on the wings of a swallow. Philomela became a nightingale.*

♫

The following Saturday Brad came over and collected Allegra in the van. He drove across Burrard bridge and up Third Avenue. When he stopped, Allegra gave no hint that she had been here before. The street was lush, the huge chestnut trees a tunnel of shade. The house itself was smaller than she remembered, and the yellow paint shabbier. As they pulled up, the door flew open and Nicky came running out, excited, full of the news that Mrs. Chan was taking him to see a movie. Mrs. Chan was a woman of forty, with red-grey hair. Nicky was a nervous four-year-old boy, a thin child, with egg-shell skin and thick black hair. As he and Mrs. Chan started downtown, Allegra found herself almost relieved she would not have to begin to get to know him this afternoon.

Then she stopped short.

The railing on one side of the front porch had been removed to make way for a plywood ramp, which stretched almost to the sidewalk, a small patch of weedy grass to be traversed in between.

Brad paused for a moment, after he'd maneuvered her onto the porch. She heard him take a deep breath, almost a sigh. He took a second breath and threw the door open, tipped the chair up and over the sill.

There were sketches and paintings everywhere, on every piece of wall, stacked on the table, on most of the chairs.

"What is this? Whose work is this?" The room simmered,

76

vibrated, jumped with energy. The first pieces she was able to take in had washes of colour over fluid ink or pencil.

"But what's this....? She pulled herself closer to a large canvas across the room. At the centre of the composition, a woman stood singing in a smoky half-lit room. The woman was tall and young and slim. She had black waist-length hair.

It was not her, and yet it was. Perhaps the face was accurate enough. She pushed herself around Brad's living room, which seemed to be given over completely to pictures of her life.

And she had told him all of this. She had told him how she had danced in a bright red dress on the night she had imagined (then) would be the saddest in her life. She had told him how she had gone off to Africa: and yes, there! more or less as she must have described it, was the tin-roofed school where swallows nested in the beams and the Harmattan blew through, where she had taught art and English and even long-division; in tiny detail she could even see the pictures the children had drawn.

And there. Two figures on the beach at Spanish Banks, just at sundown, joined in marriage by a man in a Nehru jacket—a stranger who just happened to have been passing, a tourist from Calgary—because the minister was late, and some guests had traveled thousands of miles to take part in that sunset ceremony.

Brad had taken slices of her most private moments and set them at the end of funnels.

How dare he take something so complex, open, vast? What did he know? He had one life and couldn't manage it. There it was, in the outer two thirds of these compositions. And punching through the centre of each one, that strange black shape entombing stolen scenes.

She felt her critical edge blur.

She moved towards him. She wanted to take his hand and let him know how the work gave her courage, no matter what else it made her feel. But he was looming over her.

"Don't tell anyone," he said.

He went into the dining room, where the chairs were pushed against the wall, the table covered in sketches, tin cans full of brushes, piles of paper, a roll of canvas waiting to be stretched. She followed him. He went into the kitchen, a bright high-ceilinged yellow space. She was conscious of his back, the greyish t-shirt that had been washed until it was far too small, the line of nubbled bones up his spine. When he turned, his face looked skewed and sharp, though the muscles didn't move.

He poured two glasses of wine. He helped her to her feet, and handed her the canes. She made her way over to the counter, almost tripping on the edge of a big hooked rug in front of the sink. She raised her glass and managed to hold it steady. She was about to propose a toast, but he took the glass from her hands.

He was touching her in a different, urgent way. He pulled her down onto the rug, and for once his eyes were screwed shut. A bar of sunlight struck the kitchen window, squeezed through an edge of beveled glass, making a long border of prismatic light that snaked and shifted over their tangled bodies. Allegra observed that, as she lay among the legs of chairs.

October

*A*lmost as soon as humans learned to create cloth, they began to experiment with colour. Remnants from the oldest of Egyptian tombs show traces of indigo; The Book of Exodus speaks of "curtains of blue and purple, and scarlet"; and there is even a story that the Egyptians dyed live sheep. Virgil tells us that a sheep that had been fed on the madder plant will produce red wool.

  The Phoenicians were the master dyers of the ancient world. They discovered a rare purple obtainable from small mollusk shells (murex) that were found along the coast near Tyre. Each gram of dye required some 12,000 murex shells. These small creatures have long since disappeared. Royal Purple, is the name we have given this magnificent shade....

℘

Mona does not know what she will make of all the material she has researched on the long nights of the long months, while in the days she worked in clay. Clay, unlike life, is such a forgiving medium. You can roll your creation back into a ball and dream something better into being.

She had not intended to get so caught up in myth. This is deeper water than she had imagined. She makes a note to direct her reading to more practical concerns such as how to create, for the towering figures she has pulled from clay, wings of silk in colours that are ancient, regal, Platonic ideals of the strident shades we know today.

As for herself, she has taken to wearing only white. White jeans, white shirts, white smocks, white aprons smeared with rusty clay. Not for nothing did the virgin priestesses wear white when they held the white throats of sacrificial lambs to the blade. White, she has read, holds within its brimming cup the wave-lengths of every other colour; white is not absence, white is power.

Still, night after night, words fly from the page to nest among her dreams or give new shape to memories.

§

...A fair substitute for royal purple, in ancient times, was achieved with arsenic, which produced a dye that had the added benefit of relieving the wearer of all earthly ties. It is believed that Medea got rid of Jason's interloping wife in just that way, by dipping the young princess's robe in the potent purple that went by the name of Dragon's Blood....

§

Faye has written to tell her that Brad has taken up painting. Brad. But no one is supposed to know. Faye said she learned this from Allegra Schliemann, who told it to Faye in faith.

Brad has become involved with Allegra Schliemann.

Brad has started making art.

She finds her thoughts circling back to that afternoon when she came home to find him peeling an orange, arranging the little crescents in pairs with their curved surfaces touching in a way that made them look like butterflies. He did not look up when she came in. He started flipping the pieces over, so they made half-closed circles instead.

"How come you're home so early?" she said.

"I'm not early. You're late. I started to worry. I heard on the radio there had been an accident on the bridge."

"I didn't see anything. But the traffic was certainly tied up."

"What they said on the radio was that a green Honda had been involved in a head-on collision with a van. I thought it was you."

"Okay, look," she said, "I'm sorry you were worried."

Nothing.

"Well, anyway, I'm starving," which was suddenly true.

"I stopped at the market and got some mushrooms," he said, "but I expect that's not what you want."

She dumped the mushrooms from the paper bag onto the counter, huge dark-frilled country ones. She set a pot of water on to boil for pasta, thinking, I'm leaving. I'm leaving! She poured some Tuscan oil into a pan and started slicing in the mushrooms, tears streaming from her eyes, tears of escape. When Brad came to her and put his arms around her, her skin went hot and soft with pity. He slid down to his knees. She switched off the stove.

ℂ

Legend has it that the secret of true Royal Purple was discovered by the dog of Hercules.

Hercules, as we know, was one of the many children that Zeus, the shape-changer, fathered, appearing to Leda as a swan, to Europa as a bull, to Danaë as a shower of gold, to Alcmena as her own husband, while he was away in battle—the incident that brought Hercules into being. Now Alcmena, fearing the jealousy of Hera, abandoned the infant in a field. But the goddess, who happened to be passing, heard cries of hunger and picked the baby up to give him suck, not knowing who he was. The child pulled on her breast with such strength that she threw him down in pain. Her milk flew across the sky in a scattering of stars, which became the milky way.

Some years later the youth and his dog were walking by the sea, when the dog bit into a shell-fish, then stained his master's tunic with that regal colour.

ℂ

When she had been a working weaver, Allegra had used only natural dyes. "Not many people do that anymore, not commercially," she was explaining to Brad one Saturday. "It is such a complex process."

It was easy for her to run down to the studio now, in her chair, as long as she was feeling well rested, but Brad did not approve of her on her own in this part of town.

"And I still do love those natural colours above all," she was telling him. "I hate clearing all this out." She had come down to direct Manny in the packing up of the roots and bark that filled baskets hung on pegs on the wall, dried herbs and flowers, jars of powdered lichen on the shelves. These natural ingredients exhaled softly as they were emptied into cartons and closed away.

It had taken much experimenting to find substitute dyes for printing. The ones Faye had been using at the college weren't practical for large-scale use. At first Allegra had held to the idea that it would be possible to combine her natural ones with thickeners to make a printing paste. Later she poured over many books, spent far too much on phone calls, trying to wangle secrets out of commercial operations in London, Frankfurt and New York. Finally Faye found a source, in Germany, for an ink that had a very dye-like quality, left a very soft hand (a term for the texture of printed cloth).

"Look at this, Brad." He was peering underneath the printing table, examining its construction. He couldn't believe a crew from the detox centre could produce a table so steady, so level. "Do you know what this is?"

He came over reluctantly.

"It is barberry root. You would never think that these withered chunks could produce so many shades, would you?" She flipped through a book of samples with notes attached, instructions for future dying. "These golds are what you get when you use tin as a mordant. A mordant is a chemical substance that reacts with the dye to make the colour fast and absorb into the cloth, but the choice of mordant can change the colour too. With barberry root if I change the formula slightly I get these incredible greens." The silk swatches gleamed as she fanned through them, live as serpent scales. "And here, see this wild blue. Would you believe that was extracted from carrot tops? It all depends on the mordant."

She knew he didn't care. Since her first visit to his home they had begun to settle into a routine. Brad had always had to do his artwork late at night—never on the weekend—because of Nicky's demands. When Allegra came over with a bundle of books selected from the West End library, he was able to go off into the dining room and lose himself in the world of one of his canvases, taking advantage of the light, and of her.

"If you work with lichens, for example—those crusty patches that grow on rocks?—then the most convenient mordant is ammonia," she was carrying on. "That was what made it possible, in the old days, for the crofters in Scotland to colour their own wool, and weave those wonderful tweeds. Like your jacket. I bet that's Harris tweed."

"I got it at the Sally Ann."

"Mmm," she buried her face in his chest. "I don't suppose they use the same source of ammonia anymore. In those days, an employee of the local cottage dye-works used to go around the village in the mornings to collect the night's supply of urine."

"How long are you planning to stay here today?" he said.

"This could take all afternoon. I want to make sure that all this is properly labeled, so that I can sort it out again one day."

"I thought you were going to get rid of it?"

"These ingredients have taken me *years* to collect. Some of them are very rare." She heard the bell of the front door. "Oh good, here's Faye."

"I think I'm going to leave you, then." Allegra had noticed on other occasions, too, that as soon as Faye came in Brad left. "It's not fair to Nicky to put him with a sitter on the weekends."

"What do I do?" she asked Faye, when he'd left.

Faye had sheared her splendid red hair recently, giving her pointed face a foxy look. She was working in the shadowy area at the back, sorting through sprays of dried grasses. She scratched her nose and shook her head.

"I have so much to do right now," Allegra said. "You'd think he'd understand that, especially as he gives every spare minute to his own work and resents having to give it up."

"Tell me more about Brad's painting," Faye said. She was looping strands of eel grass, tying them into obedient knots before arranging them in a shoe box. Ferragamo. Where on earth had they got that? "Is his painting good? Or just...decorative?"

Allegra laughed. She and Faye had often gone over to Granville Street and done the Art Walk, when Allegra had more energy. They had fine arguments about what was good and what was not."

"I don't really know," Allegra said. "The subject matter is me," she admitted now. "So it's difficult to judge."

"What? Portraits?"

"Hard to explain. He does pictures within pictures, tiny detailed scenes that make me think of ships in bottles. Do you know how they get them in there—those schooners with all the masts and sails—how that's done?"

"My dad used to do that. You build them first, and to slide them in you *flatten* them."

She would have liked to ask Faye what Brad had been like with Mona. But she was sure Faye kept the two friendships separate.

Mona.

The question of Mona had seemed simple at first. A fine and admirable artist, who as luck would have it had decided quite on her own to leave. A compelling person, easy to like. Allegra remembered a long discussion they'd once had, at some gallery opening, though now she had no recollection of what the subject had been.

Sometimes, lately, she imagined Mona's thoughts braiding into her own. Could you lie next to the skin of someone who had lain with someone else, and not pick up a residue of thoughts breathed into the crevices and folds?

℘

The appliquéed placemats had been surprisingly successful. Many stores had ordered them for Christmas but before the mats could be delivered, the seamstresses had to be paid.

Then FibreWorks got its first genuine high-fashion commission, thanks to a connection of Jim's in New York, who—on the strength of designs by Faye—was prepared to pay genuine New York dollars for a coordinating collection of printed silk for next fall's line. The studio was to start with a hundred yards of each of three designs, each pattern in four colourways; there would be much more to follow if this worked out. The deadline was February.

℘

Every night, when she went home—ignoring Brad's advice and wheeling on her own, taking the route through Gastown—she would open her cupboard door to swing out her vertical loom. It seemed essential, during those days, to do as much on the tapestry as she could. Strangely, Brad's paintings pushed her along: the way he had her down so accurately, yet always got it wrong. That precious detail, that slickness. She had to set the record straight, the only way she could and as crude as her work must be now. A flame pattern had taken over lately which seemed to grow quite naturally around the creamy flower in the centre.

She kept expecting a call from the man on the seawall. When she didn't hear, she took out his card. No telephone number. Odd. She looked for him in the phone book. No one listed by that name. Directory Assistance was no help. She ran her fingers over the heavy wine-coloured letters on the card. The embossed script looped and trailed, making a beguiling design on its own. But there seemed no way for her to track down George DiSemele or his clinic.

§

The results of the tests with the new dyes were glowing but subtle. The thickness of the print-paste added an interesting dimension, as if the fabric were embossed. Despite the worries, as the preparations crept along, Allegra found that she could hardly sleep at night for seeing patterns, for picturing the beautiful yardage they would produce, exclusive, expensive, carriage trade.

One concern with the German inks was that they had to be heated to a very specific temperature (curing this was called), or else when the fabric was washed or even dry-cleaned the pattern would float away. Special machines were manufactured to do this; the one Allegra had her eye on cost thousands of dollars. She and Faye cured the test samples by standing over them with an iron. The inks released dreadful fumes.

Each colour of pigment was sold only by the fifty gallon drum, requiring huge investment even if they ordered only the three primary colours. Allegra pondered all of this as she supervised the boys from the college stretching the canvas over the padded table. The cloth had to be stretched absolutely tight, so the fabric to be printed would be smoothed onto it. She was calculating how much she would need to borrow, how much further she could extend their line of credit, when Jim came back from lunch. They had been lovers first, friends always.

"Jim, you've been in sales all your life. Tell me what to do."

He hunched forward, his red beard bristling. "Have you thought of selling the dye before it gets here, to give you the money to pay for it when it arrives?"

"Go into the dye business, you mean?"

"Who better? Why not?"

The sound of firecrackers in the lane, the smell of gunpowder in the air. They were going into battle—wits sharpened, flags flying, leaders of a small brave crew of renegade entrepreneurs. They sat down and worked out the details: Jim would use the samples they already had to go around to craft shops, t-shirt printers, art shops, to take orders, so they could take those to the bank. Then from Germany they would buy just the colourless base and the primary colours, from which Allegra could mix the entire spectrum, keeping half of what they purchased for their own use, selling the rest in small attractive bottles, with their label, for ten times what they had paid.

Even the name came to them. "Halcyon," Jim said. "It has positive connotations."

"As in halcyon days? Lets look it up."

"One," she read out. "A bird anciently fabled to breed about the time of the winter solstice in a nest floating on the sea, said to charm the wind and waves so that the sea was specially calm; usually identified with a species of kingfisher."

"Two: Calm, quietude, halcyon days."

An ash can exploded in the lane.

"Three: A bird known for its propensity *to take a dive*."

"Are dictionaries usually humourous?" she wondered.

℘

Like Zeus, colour is a shape-changer, doing all it can to make us see an effect that is not there. Put blue and yellow side-by-side, and the blue will become violet, the yellow will edge to orange. Modern theorists have written volumes on colour's properties; but these have certainly been understood since the Middle Ages, or long before, enabling the medieval tapestry-weaver to create shimmering results using yarns of far fewer individual colours than those we think we see.

The subtlety of medieval tapestries cannot be duplicated today with chemical dyes; and for the most part we have lost the antique recipes. We know that Gioanventura Rosetti of Venice, after fifteen years of research, published one of the first books on dyeing, The Plictho, *which included formulas for the famed Venetian reds and blacks. We do not have access to it, here. Another 16th century Italian recipe involves iron filings, eggshells, grindings from oak galls, roche alum, and a good measure of lye.*

To create green on the other hand, that classic shade of jealousy, one needs to boil red vinegar, along with filings of copper and brass, then add vitriol and verdigris. This produces "a green so strong that never more it will go away."

℘

One day Brad surprised Allegra by coming by the studio after work. FibreWorks looked efficient, compared with the last time he'd come. He looked efficient himself in a pair of crisp new Acme Glass overalls, blue-and-white striped, with the logo embroidered on the bib.

"Come on," she said, "I'll show you the inner sanctum."

No one was to know the secret of how they composed their dyes, not even the students who came to work there; but of course that did not apply to Brad. She took him along to the room they'd closed off at the back, and unlocked the door.

As soon as the drums of pigment had arrived, the name of the manufacturer had been spray-painted over and the FibreWorks logo stencilled on. In the shop at the front, where the weavings used to be, the shelves were stocked with glass-stoppered dye bottles so pretty they might have been designed for perfume. In the secret room behind, the walls were papered with sheets dabbed with colour, scribbled with formulas, percentages used in combinations of yellow, red and blue to achieve the rainbow of Halcyon shades.

"So what do you think of our operation?"

Jim came in with a carton of the glass vials he began to unpack onto the work bench. He and Brad nodded. Allegra had never heard them exchange a word.

"You need a fan in here. Do you know what you're breathing in?"

"We're getting one." She could see he was getting claustrophobic. "Soon we'll have to move, of course. I have my eye on a place at Granville Island that has huge windows and twice the space."

She led him out to the main work area, now dominated by the printing table that stretched end to end of the long room. "I want to show you the mechanics of registering the screens."

Jim edged by with a tray of filled bottles to take to the front. Brad made a half step to the side.

"This has to be exact," she said. "Think what this table is designed to do. We take a bolt of white cloth and it has to end up being one long continuous design, fitting together perfectly, like a puzzle. This requires a lot of mathematical figuring. You have to calculate where to set down each screen, so that in the end it all interlocks.

Since he'd last been here all the roots and herbs and even the baskets had been sold to a craft shop out in Surrey—she'd had to do that in the end, to generate some extra cash—and this entire streamlined printing system installed. She had even managed to locate a curing machine that a bankrupt t-shirt company had been getting rid of.

"The bolt of fabric gets unrolled bit by bit onto this conveyor belt," she said, "and moves through the heat box. You can adjust both the heat, and the speed, to get the right combination, depending on what the fabric is. For example, when we do the silk it will have to be at a lower temperature, so the belt will be slowed down."

He had been silent for so long that she understood that something was wrong.

"How did you afford all this?" he asked.

"You know we have one of those Apprenticeship-Training grants that helps pay the wage of Manny and the other detox guys. And Faye has a whole crew of students who come and work on spec, because once we get going they will all have jobs."

"Doesn't it strike you as a bit risky, making all these promises to kids who are probably already up to their necks in student loans?"

"What is this? What's going on with you today?"

"And your former partner?"

"Jim?"

"If that's his name."

"Jim has decided to come back and help us get this going. He's a good businessman. He knows the ropes, how to deal with the banks. I don't have time for all of that right now."

"So you have borrowed for all of this?"

"Not exactly. There was a little money left to me by my aunt. Not much, but I had been saving it for a time when I couldn't work."

"And you put it all into this?"

"I don't understand. What's wrong with you? What's wrong, in general."

"I think you ought to look ahead, that's all."

"What are you saying? Brad, this is what fuels me, this *is* my future—and this is what is going to make me well."

"You're down here at all hours."

"Why not? I never know when you're coming by."

"You know my situation."

"And you know mine. I wish you could share some of my excitement. What's the point if we can't share these things?"

"There's no point, if you are so stubborn you won't listen. How can you possibly expect this to pay off? You've spent a fortune."

"Oh, you are absolutely right. It's crazy."

He looked surprised.

"But I believe in it, just as I believe that I am going to beat this damned disease. I have to believe in that, what's the alternative? Well, this is an act of faith as well."

November

*L*ike *childrens' puzzles in activity books, where bicycles and rabbits and fire engines and lions have concealed themselves in the tops of trees or in the ripples on a pond, the most effective patterns do not give up their secrets at a glance. Think of "magic blocks", a design found on patchwork quilts, Navajo rugs, antique embroidered Chinese robes, where an arrangement of box shapes will turn upside down before your eyes, drum itself into a diagonal flight as solid as a set of stairs, only to flip, to become a succession of hollow hanging cubes.*

Even the most straight-forward pattern contains beneath its surface the potential of surprise. Light alternates with dark. Green flicks to red. A face pops out of the abstract motifs on a Shang vase, and the t'ao-t'tieh appears, an heraldic animal which, like the dragon, the griffin, will shortly begin its long procession through the centuries.

To see the secret life of pattern, it is best to have the artless attention of a child.

§⌒

Brad was working on a tiny scene that showed a woman in a mirrored tower. She was looking out through the reflection, gazing at sky, mountains, sea. The window was twined with ivy, twined with vines bearing small heart-shaped tomatoes, some shown sliced open, the seeds varnished gold. She was leaning on canes. There were carved eagles on the canes.

He was thinking that although Allegra said little about his work—sometimes her expression when she watched was strange—his dread of letting her see what he'd been doing had not been justified. Her understanding, her looking, had confirmed his work was real.

In the beginning he had told himself he was attracted to her life, to all that swam around her in the air. He studied the way she moved her hands and tossed her head. He followed stories she spun from the threads of the most ordinary lives, trailing her deep into the minds of people she had known, not a voyeur but an explorer. It had been a fine adventurous feeling as he lay back on her cushioned couch watching her, the lines of her face becoming as quick and automatic to him as a signature.

"All the same, you don't have to idealize me," she had said to him not long ago. "All those scenes from my past. I'd like to think there is some value in my present condition, too."

He had looked at her lovely face, which on some days, in some lights, was ruined. But it doesn't matter, he had wanted to say. He was wise enough to keep quiet. There was much she didn't know.

℘

She called him early Saturday morning.

"Brad, we have an emergency. I don't think I'll be able to come over. In fact, I was wondering if I could borrow your van—and borrow you. It's a long story. *The Beaver Express* van was stolen, while it was delivering our mats...."

The van had been stolen from in front of Starbucks before the driver made any of his calls. Their entire Christmas line vanished along with the van.

"That was why I was preoccupied when you called yesterday."

"I thought you told me the stores were expecting the mats in the middle of last month."

"It took much longer to get them finished than we'd expected. Some of the women were very slow, and one of them ruined a whole order by using the wrong colour thread. We had to get them done over again by someone else. I didn't want to bother you with all that."

"And now they've all been stolen."

"That's what I said."

He carried the phone on its long cord over to his easel and added small dots of carnelian to the shadows in the hollows of the wood of her eagle canes.

"What do you expect me to do?"

"Well they've found the van. It was ditched in Richmond. It's been towed to a body shop out there, and our mats are safe! But, I've got to get them delivered to the stores today. I've called all the shops. They've already been delayed and delayed."

He stepped back and looked at his painting. Behind the outline of the funnel, he had painted his son in motion kicking a red ball, just his legs and feet with their blue shoes, filling the background.

"So what am I supposed to do with Nick?"

"Oh Brad, thank you so much. Bring Nick along. He'll get a chance to meet a real policeman. You'll have to go to the station before they'll let you take the mats, but I've phoned and they're expecting you."

෴

"Allegra, look, look!" Nicky broke away from Brad and ran into the shop. "They gave me a police hat! They're the ones the Mounties wear. See it's got the crest on the front."

Nicky had made good use of his hat all afternoon, marching ahead of Brad into places that otherwise would surely have been snooty, as Brad, still in his painting jeans, staggered into rooms full of crystal, china, gleaming silver and stainless steel, carrying bulky brown-wrapped packages. In every shop, the women in charge bent their taut backs and patted Nicky on the head before examining the invoice. A couple of them even wrote out cheques then and there, though they could have waited thirty days.

They all remarked that FibreWorks' presentation had been excellent. Inside the brown wrapper was a second layer which had been printed with their logo, over and over, a web within a circle, done in gold.

"Brad thank you so much. Was it awful? You look tired."

"Yes, but *you* look tired," he said. "What's going on?"

"Oh we've had a crazy day. It's nothing."

The phone rang.

"Hang on."

When she made her way over to answer it, he was aware of how everyone in the place paused and waited.

"So what's the verdict?" Jim's girlfriend Asia said. She pronounced it "voidict".

Allegra shook her head. "No news."

"We think our order of silk is lost at sea," she said. "Not just the silk. The whole boat seems to have disappeared. They think it may have been hi-jacked. I've just been talking to the RCMP..."

Nicky popped up and saluted.

"...the International Crime division, who have somehow become involved. I've been faxing back and forth to Mr. Chan in China, all week. Of course their government is trying to track it down as well, otherwise the China Silk Corporation won't get paid."

"Hang on, I don't understand. I thought you had that all under control long ago. Aren't you all set to start the printing? Didn't you tell me last week that you have a big order from back east?"

"Yes, but I didn't want to worry you,"

"So now it's my fault that I'm so easily worried? That's why you never tell me anything?"

"Is this going to turn out to be all about you?"

Allegra was white with exhaustion.

"Look, I'm sorry. I know it's bad news that you haven't received the silk yet. Couldn't you go out and buy some here, so you could get started on the designs?"

"Even if we could get it, it would make our work prohibitively expensive. No, we'll have to rely on the Chinese to track it down."

"What can be so important about your order that would make

both the RCMP and the Chinese government want to get involved?"

"A lot of money is at stake. Even at wholesale, the silk we ordered costs...." Her voice trailed off. He remembered she'd boasted that they could get it for less than a dollar a yard. Obviously this figure had climbed. "And then, you see," she continued, "to buy from them at all, we're required to meet enormous minimums."

"Like what?"

"Actually the least you can buy is two hundred thousand."

"Two hundred thousand what?"

"Yards."

So they were going to sell what they didn't need to pay for the whole order, she was explaining rapidly. They had sold it already, mainly. That had been Jim's idea, to finance the silk the same way they had financed the dyes.

"And if it doesn't arrive?"

"It's insured. They will send us another order. But, first they have to determine what has happened to the original shipment. Typical bureaucratic stuff. They have to determine that it's lost, and to do that they have to find it. The problem is, we have to start printing,."

"Come on, I'll take you out to dinner. What do you say?"

∞

They got to the Pink Pearl before the Saturday evening lineup. Nicky wanted chicken wings and egg-roll and chocolate milk. He had been here for Dim Sum once or twice and wanted to know where the food carts were. They ordered his favourites and also black bean shrimp, steamed fish with bean curd, deep-fried wanton, and Allegra asked for greens.

"I think I need some iron. Something."

She looked so crumpled that Brad found himself remembering a flower that he had found in an old book of his mother's, when he was a boy. There was an illustration of a knight in armour on the front; but the book was all in a language he didn't understand. As he was sliding it back into the glass-fronted bookcase, a white rose had fallen out, papery, ancient, but still trailing a faint smell. When his mother came home she found the pressed flower on the floor and she sat down in her chair and started to cry.

Nicky ate his egg roll and then slipped to the floor to play with two boys from the next table. They were shy, but impressed with his hat, and soon they were sharing their Leggo despite the fact they were languages apart.

Allegra's greens came. "I'm afraid you'll have to cut these up for me." She couldn't manage chopsticks now; she had to lift everything with a fork and even that was hard. "Do you hate doing this?"

"Of course not." Brad tossed the mustard greens with soy sauce, squared them off into bite-sized chunks.

"Then why so serious?"

"I was thinking about something that happened when I was a boy," he said quickly.

"When you were a boy?" Every trace of tiredness now gone.

He told her about his mother's rose.

"Maybe your mother's tears really did rejuvenate that flower." Her forehead crinkled. "Your mother wept years ago, but the rose did not come alive for you till now."

"You're making my head spin."

"But listen. I've been thinking about this a lot. Thinking about you. About your parents. How there seem to be so many things you never want to talk about."

He banged the table so hard Nicky's chocolate milk tipped off onto the floor. "Can't you ever leave me alone?"

§)

Perhaps he would have stormed out right then, if it hadn't been for Nicky and his friends crawling out to look at the mess, and the boys' parents pulling back their chairs, offering napkins with alarmed but sympathetic smiles. He sopped up the mess on the carpet, dabbed his jeans. Allegra watched all of this, very still. He caught a current of what her anger had been like over on the island, how it had swept him beyond caution, exposed his secret life. He had a confused impression of power in her growing from the rocks of the earth. A woman who now could barely walk. Overpowering, implacable.

He sat down and twirled his wine glass. She was watching him. The glass was sticky. His hands were sticky.

"When I was a little, my mother used to tell me stories," he finally said. "She used to close my bedroom door, so my dad wouldn't hear, and sit on the edge of my bed and smooth my hair...."

§)

His mother put on a dreamy sing-song voice so that he half knew she was telling the story to herself.

"Once there was a girl with raven hair and she lived in a mansion on the edge of the forest, and every night she went to her window because she hoped her love would come to her. He was a bold man, a great man, and the people worshiped him. He rode a white horse through the villages, carrying a sword in one hand and a religious icon in the other. The people of the countryside called him The Captain. They believed that he had been sent to save them."

But the spies of the king were always watching. The king had fallen under the spell of a wicked woman. No one was to know that the young girl's father was the Captain's blood brother, that the mansion was the meeting place of a secret brotherhood who wore crosses and packets of Romanian soil around their necks and had sworn to free the Fatherland.

Late at night, when the meeting in the house was over, the Captain lead his horse beneath the young girl's window and lifted her down to him so together they would ride through the darkened forest to a nearby hilltop and he would show her the stars....

"And then did they get married?"

"Ah no. There is a witch in this story, and she prevented that."

"So what happened to the Captain?"

"The Captain was murdered by agents of the king. The king would have murdered the girl's father too, if it had not been for that pact of secrecy. So two years later, after the king had fled the country, the father was able to avenge the Captain's death."

"And then what?"

"Ah then, though the father of the girl fought bravely, he himself was killed. But the girl grew up and crossed the ocean, where she received a gift beyond compare."

"What was that?"

"The gift of a son, *fiule*, my little one...."

Brad wanted to hear about the man on the white horse, about his sword and how he fought, about his murder and about how those men became blood brothers. His mother always dwelt on the business of the stars.

Sometimes, he would play the part of the Captain. He'd go out in the backyard and gallop around and make up variations of the story, because of course he knew the girl's father was Brad's grandfather, though his mother never said so. His own grandfather had been a hero, a sword-wielding member of a secret brotherhood!

But one day, when Brad was eight years old, he spent the whole day sick in his mother's bed, while she was at work. He found himself staring at the wooden chest that stood on her dresser. He'd never seen inside it. Once when he'd come running in, she'd slammed it shut and turned the key.

Where did she keep the key?

A loose floor-board underneath a corner of the carpet? The top shelf of the wardrobe, behind the hat-box? Brad searched all the difficult-to-get-to places first, but eventually, in a drawer where she kept all the lacy things, he came upon a small enameled box held closed by a rubber band. Precious things: earrings, a broach made out of a circle of garnetts with an arrow running through, a small brass key.

The key turned sweetly in the lock. But what a disappointment. Just a bunch of old papers and letters in that language Brad couldn't read. Then (but he heard a car door slam, his mother's laugh out on the sidewalk) he saw there was another compartment underneath. He peered in and saw something brown and lumpy on the dark blue velvet, which, for a second, he thought was a dead mouse. It was a small leather pouch held closed by a thong.

The bag was full of caked dry earth. *The secret brotherhood.* Every night Brad got it out and looked at it and told himself stories of the brave things his grandfather had done, until one day, something prompted him to take it to school for Show and Tell.

§

Brad didn't tell Allegra everything. Most, but not the worst.

Still, she was shaking her head. She had come from the studio wearing an old shirt that had a pattern of vine leaves. He was wondering if she'd buttoned it up wrong or if the shirt had been manufactured carelessly; it didn't match at the front. The waiter set down a plate of fortune cookies with the bill underneath.

He wished she would stop looking at him. She would never understand how it felt to be trailed by suspicions about your origins, alert to the moment when a wash of evil would steal over you, a wave so dazzling that in one crucial instant you might do something dreadful, quite certain that it was right, heroic.

§

The following weekend he took on the project of painting her kitchen cupboards, which he remembered she had wanted to have done when they first met. She was all buttoned up in her duffel coat and ready to leave for his place when he arrived with paint, brushes, varsol, rollers and rags.

"But how did you know I hadn't changed my mind? Maybe I won't like the colour?"

"It's ox-blood," he said. "The same colour you were talking about. You had a chip of it, remember?"

It was a cloudy day but not raining, not even cold. After a while

Allegra said it would probably be better if she took Nicky out, so they wouldn't have to breathe the fumes.

"Here." She tied a long piece of red ribbon to the arm of her motorized wheel chair. "If we go over to the aquarium, Nick, will you promise to hang onto this—that you will never leave my chair?"

Nicky promised. She called a cab.

The phone rang endlessly. Half lost in thought, he reached out to grab the receiver, forgetting the machine.

A foreign voice, deep, with a thin layer of charm. A salesman, probably. When Brad said Allegra was out, the man was not willing to let well enough alone.

"Is it not correct that she carries a cell phone?"

Brad found himself saying he didn't know.

The man insisted on leaving his name and number, urging Brad to get Allegra to call him back. Brad wrote the number on the newspaper underneath his paint can. When he was cleaning up, he threw it out with the debris. He forgot to tell Allegra about the call.

December

Queen Semiramis, the mythical Assyrian, was noted for her beauty and wisdom. She conquered many lands. She founded the city of Babylon. She conquered Egypt and established the cultivation of cotton along the Nile. After a long and prosperous life she vanished from the earth in the shape of a dove.

It was fortunate that Semiramis came up with cotton, mythical or not, for Egyptian law restricted the use of wool. Members of the priesthood were forbidden to wear it next to their skin. Herodotus tells us the Assyrians were governed by similar laws.

As to the wearing of silk, that was controlled less by law than by secrecy. For thousands of years its production was a closely guarded secret of the Chinese. Tradition sets its discovery at about 2600 B.C., when a certain Emperor of

China asked his wife to discern the origins of a blight that was destroying his mulberry trees. She found the leaves being eaten by worms that spun glossy cocoons. Thanks to the merest accident she dropped one of these in a basin of hot water, then in amazement watched as the cocoon separated into a network of delicate fibers which she was able to pull, and pull, and pull, into a long continuous filament. Not for three thousand years was the secret of silk production smuggled to the west. Two Nestorian monks—agents of the Ottoman Emperor Justinian—made their way back from China with silk worm eggs hidden in their hollow walking sticks. Silk has a long history of deceit and subterfuge.

§

Allegra made her way down to Cordova Street. All the store-fronts were glass boxes full of light. Christmas music leaked onto the street from every door. The sky was slate and cold. She moved in and out of pools of brilliance, pools of dusk. She should have been down at the studio hours ago. She'd had trouble getting on her boots, which had surprised her, because she had managed perfectly well yesterday: as if overnight her feet had swelled to double size and her hands had turned to fins. Eventually she'd given up and stuffed her feet into an old pair of fur-lined leather moccasins.

Yesterday she'd had an appointment with Dr. Walgren, a specialist she had waited six months to see.

A man with eyes like thin worn dimes.

He had told her that because she had never been in remission, there was no reason to expect one now. He had suggested coldly that she ought to be looking ahead to finding a place in a long-term care facility—that she certainly should not expect the government to supply the home-care she would need.

In the elevator up to her apartment she had jammed her gears. She had ridden the lift back down to the basement where it picked up another tenant—the kind East Indian man from the fourth floor—who came up with her and helped her in. She sat in the dark, needing desperately to go to the bathroom, but unable to move. She realized she had left her canes at the doctor's when she fled. She tried to heave herself out of her chair. Then it was too late.

She reached for the pair of pointed barber's scissors by the sink, quite calmly. She had crossed a line. She could not take another painful breath. But when she tried to pick the scissors up, they slipped to the floor.

Brad came in and found her.

Like one who has survived a shipwreck she accepted his help, knowing the turn they had taken. He was no longer her lover. Desire cringes in the face of such distress.

He went to her drawer and selected a high-necked flannel nightgown. He did up every button, carried her to bed.

Then he lay down beside her and undid all the buttons again.

§⁊

The street atmosphere changed as she got further along Hastings, down to the block where Woodwards used to be, the windows papered from inside, the only place still in business was the army surplus across the way. She cut down towards Cordova. The fresh air had revived her, she was having no trouble now with the controls. In Gastown, a big tree was set up near the steam clock, a busker on the street playing carols on a comb.

When she got to the studio, the whole crew was standing around. Jim had just put down the phone. Their broker had received confirmation that a replacement order of silk had been sent off. It would arrive sometime in January.

Faye said. "Shall we call the designer and say we will be a little late but that it's all under control?"

"Not yet." Allegra was surprised how calm she felt.

"Let's prepare every design, every screen," she said. "Then we will print each one on rolls of newsprint. We will do every scrap of preparation before Christmas. This will give us a head start. The designer will receive everything in good order. He will make masterpieces, not the Emperor's new clothes."

∽

The mention of sumptuary laws among the Assyrians and Egyptians brings us around to the purposes of clothes. Not as straight-forward as first appears.

Eve sewed fig leaves together and made aprons to cover up their shame (Genesis 3:7.21) but we have early evidence of a far more diverse role that clothing played: not just to appease the deities and cover shame, but to invoke magic, to bring about fertility, to protect against evil—and to satisfy a deep human craving for decoration.

Why else would we have discovered, in burial sites dating back hundreds of thousands of years, those brilliant beads spread out in complex patterns over crumbling skeletons, decoration once sewn into garments that have long since rotted away. So strong is the urge toward personal adornment that it has blossomed in every country in every age. And too in every age a bureaucracy blooms to control it. Of course the ruling classes in most countries have been able to ignore such laws, often coming up with unusual uses for their exotic clothes. In Tutankhamen's tomb, for example, archaeologists discovered sandals painted with pictures of tied-up captives on the soles, so that with every step the Pharaoh could tread upon his enemies.

§

Allegra woke to the sound of Christmas Carols on her bedside radio. On her way home from the studio the day before she had passed a used clothing store that displayed an ankle-length coat of dark, rich fur that gave even the too-pink mannequin the glow of a Russian princess. She bought it and a high-crowned red leather hat. Merely possessing such garments seemed a talisman; hardly any need to wear them. She *would* wear them, sometime before Christmas, when they went out for a festive meal.

They had not talked of the holidays at all, but she had begun picturing how she and Brad and Nicky would all wake up at Brad's on Christmas Day. She still had not spent a night in Brad's bed. Their intimacy was such now that Brad's scruples, about Nicky, struck her as absurd. Brad had started doing a series based on her younger days. Recently she'd offered him a story each time they got together, a little gift, a bauble, something so pretty you could hang it on a tree. She shaped her stories, now, before she handed them over, shined them up, did everything she could to please. *Little harlot stories.* As if that glamorous other creature, her perfected younger self, would both keep him satisfied and keep him close. Those were the sort of bargains you had to make with yourself, she supposed. Women made worse, every day.

She lay longer than she should have in the flowery bedroom

alcove, listening to the radio, reflecting on how she had created this space for herself when she first moved into this apartment, when she'd imagined that from that time forward she would sleep alone. She studied the red-flowered curtains, the small echoing sprigs on the sheets and quilt, trying to work out exactly how the pattern repeated, how she would set about designing such a print. What a fine sense of order a clever pattern could bestow, a gridwork underneath all the bare spots of your life.

She began thinking about her tapestry again, drifting into sleep. The design she was trying to weave became a great puzzle. *Simple,* a voice pronounced, *just find the square root of red.* She stirred to the sound of Christmas music and roused herself to plan the day.

Yesterday she had stopped by the Good Will on Davie and bought a Monopoly set, complete except for a pair of dice. She would ask Nicky to make some out of sugar cubes. He was a handful: jumping on the sofa as if it was a trampoline; leaping from chair to chair around the room, so that almost every time he'd fall; beating that little drum she'd been fool enough to buy for him.

By the time Brad arrived it had started raining. Nicky had been promised a trip to the petting zoo at Stanley Park, and now that was impossible.

"Nicky, I wish you wouldn't do that."

While Allegra was collecting her things, he'd started twisting up the macramé rope on the pot that held her spider plant, winding it tighter and tighter, and then letting it go, so the plant went spinning. The rope was sure to break. He was winding up the rope again, his small white face blinkered to the dreariness of a rainy day and an apartment full of things he was not allowed to touch.

Brad was flipping through her books, ignoring her look of

appeal. She stared into her mirrored walls, amid all the busy objects in her room. It took her a moment to find herself. She rummaged in her chest of drawers until she found a mohair shawl that she had woven long ago in stripes of plum and saffron and amethyst and the deep purple-brown she had extracted from choke-cherry bark. She wrapped herself in a cloud of that warm colour.

℘

Long after the instructions in Exodus setting forth what priests in their temples were allowed to wear (only pure linen), or the further proscription against garments of mixed fibres found in Deuteronomy, or the details regarding what weavers were forbidden to do (sing at their work) and what they had to wear (a woolen plug in the ear) or the prohibition against a married woman's spinning in the street, or in the open, or absolutely anywhere by moonlight lest her arms be revealed—centuries after all of this, and skimming for the moment over the injunctions against various types of garments in countries of the Orient (all of which rather than cutting back extravagance, as hoped, merely caused spurts of invention), we will settle for a moment in Medieval Italy.

"What does a woman's train stir up, when she walks on the road?" asked San Bernardino as he preached in Siena. "Dust—and in the winter it wallows in the mud. And the person who walks behind her in summer breathes the incense she has stirred up, and that is called the devil's incense!" He went so far as to turn his venom on her hats. "I know women who have more heads than the devil...I see some who wear them in the shape of tripe, and some like a pancake, some like a trencher...some folded up and some turned down. Could you but see yourselves, you look like so many owls and hawks! O women, you have made a God of your head!"

§

As Brad helped her into his living room she noticed that the old-fashioned room would take a good tall tree. She started to imagine the gold-sprayed wreaths made out of weeds, the strings of cranberries, the gilded corn-cob angel for the tree.

She noticed how empty the room really was. Not empty of clutter, not empty of canvasses and sketches and jars of brushes and piles of paperback books, and bits of toys: but empty of its former life, empty of Brad's former life. There was not a photo to disturb the illusion that this had always been a single-parent home. Not a picture of Mona, anywhere. Not even a snapshot of Brad—no photo albums from when he was growing up, no baby pictures, no high-school yearbooks. The place had the frayed, neglected look of bachelorhood. Brad had been so determined to fix up her place, but here even the chimney was stopped up, so they could never have a fire.

"Look," Brad said, "I just want to finish what I started last night. I won't be long."

"Do you have any pictures of when you were a kid?" she asked. "It's a perfect day for looking at old snapshots."

"What for?"

"Just to know you better." She gestured around her. "You know every single thing about me!"

"It's all in a trunk somewhere. I guess. And Nicky, no! You can't watch T.V."

"Come on, let's make some cocoa," Allegra said. "After that we'll play Monopoly."

Getting Nicky's help was more effort than doing it herself,

except that she couldn't do it herself, and he could heat the milk in a heavy saucepan, measure in the Nestle's Quick from the fat, brown, plastic bear, carefully ladle out the cocoa from the pot into the jug. He carried in the jug into the living room and set it on the lid of an old wicker box beside the couch. He was just returning with the tray of mugs, when Brad came in from the other room. "Don't put that there!"

"We're being careful, Dad."

"I've told you before. Any liquid that gets spilled on that will drip right through those little holes." He shoved a pile of books off the table in front of the fireplace and moved the whole tray over there. Allegra looked carefully at the box. It was fastened with an old-fashioned iron lock.

"What do you keep in there?" she asked.

"I've lost the key. But if it gets things spilled in it, we'll have mice or ants."

"What is in there?" she whispered to Nicky, when his father had returned to the other room.

He shrugged. "Stuff that used to be my grandma's?"

Something he didn't want Allegra to see. Letters from Mona?

She pulled her mohair shawl around her and began to speculate.

℘

Forbidden fabrics in Florence, in the thirteenth century, included all multi-coloured cloth, including stripes and checks, as well as "embossed velvet, brocade, samite, and rich embroideries in gold and silver." But when the authorities burst in and started going through the cupboards of a certain noble home, it is recorded that they discovered "a gown of white marbled silk, with vine leaves and red grapes, lined with striped white cloth—a cote with red and white roses on a pale yellow ground—a gown of blue cloth with white lilies and white and red stars and compasses, and white and yellow silken stripes across it, lined with striped red cloth..." However the lady of the house was somewhat short on underclothes. Four shifts of fine white linen. No under-drawers. No nightgown. She and her husband both had night-caps to wear to bed.

§

Allegra pushed her wheelchair through into the kitchen and turned on the radio. More Christmas carols. In the other room, Nicky was bouncing around from chair to chair.

"Nick," she called, "come and help me make some lunch." She hiked herself up with her canes and started peering through the cupboard. Noodle soup.

"See if you can drive this electric can-opener, okay?" Sometimes she could get such a lovely smile out of him.

"Right—now into the pot and add a can of water." A lot of noodles on the counter. "Now stir it up. Then you can make some toast."

Nicky bent his head right over toaster, trying to see when it would pop. When the toast hit him on the nose, he wanted to make more and more.

Once the soup was on its way, she went through to the living room to see what Brad was doing. She came around the corner and caught him at his work. He stood with his shoulders hunched, his tall body bent, as he mixed colour in a small saucer that he held in his palm. With the finest of brushes he transferred this to the canvas: strokes that were no more than the movement of two fingers, his hand held rigid with the discipline of the tiny scene's demands. When she saw him like that, her heart sank with the enormous freight of love.

A crash from the kitchen. Nicky was cowering in the far corner. A bottle that had been on the window sill was a now a mess of jagged purple glass on the floor. Nicky's feet were bare. His small toes curled inward.

"Are you okay?"

"I gave that to Mum, once, for Mother's Day." He was sobbing.

Allegra pulled herself up by holding tight to her chair. "Here, take my hand. Step up over." She wanted to take him in her arms.

Brad appeared at the door. "Come on Nick, don't overdo it."

"But I gave that to Mum. How am I ever going to tell her, at Christmas, that I broke her favourite thing?"

"Is your mum coming home for Christmas?"

Allegra was glad that her voice was muffled. She felt the beat of his chest against hers, fast and fragile as a bird's.

"Well, she will just be glad to see you. She won't mind that you broke it."

"Dad paid a lot of money for that."

Allegra couldn't look at Brad.

"Come on, I think the best thing we can do right now is make ourselves invisible," she said, scooping Nicky up onto her lap in the chair. She spun the wheels and headed into the bathroom and locked the door, Nicky gaping in surprise.

"Invisible? How?"

She started fishing in the bag at the side of her chair. She found her makeup bag, full of tubes of greasy eye shadow and lipsticks.

"Put on some protective covering. A mask. Something to fool

your dad completely. What do you say?"

Brad had swept up all the glass, when they came out. "We haven't the faintest idea what happened to Nicky and Allegra," Allegra said. "But we want ice cream."

"Yes, ice cream," Nicky said. A small faltering voice, still not sure where all of this was going. "Or we will eat you up!"

"Just like we ate up Nicky," Allegra said.

Brad turned to the fridge. Allegra grabbed her things and headed for the door, not even bothering to remove the make-up.

§

The blue flush, the blue flame, whatever had once propelled her when she ran, infused her now. The streets were icy but she didn't skid. Her sleek chair flew forward. She remembered the admiring stranger on the sea wall. Why had he not called?

She took backstreets at first so Brad would not find her if he came after her, and then zoomed straight down the hill to Cornwall. The day had turned clear, magnificent. Light sliced along the sides of houses, beat iron shapes out of the filigree of branches, the bare trunks of trees. She was wearing just her shawl, but she wasn't cold. How much energy this released, when a sliver of ice pierced your heart.

As she waited at the light on Cornwall before making the street-crossing over to the bridge—where she would have to maneuver the various curb cuts with the chair tilting precariously, the traffic dangerous and impatient if she got caught half way across—she began to have the sense of being in a spiral. That flame of anger leaping up, and then subsiding leaving just a residue of shame. Over and over in her life. Always it came from a slightly new direction, but the pattern repeated again and again. She began the long arc over the bridge, in the chill wind.

A few leaves still shivered on the poplars. There was new snow on the mountains, the strait was galloping with white-capped waves. Everything was a sudden unexpected blaze of blue and white and gold, late that same afternoon. Allegra had been standing on her balcony for a long time, leaning on the rail. She heard Brad let himself into her apartment. She didn't turn.

"Come inside." He carried her to the couch and settled her among the cushions. He poured her a glass of wine. "I didn't hear you leave. What is this? What's going on?"

"I think we should stop seeing each other. This is going nowhere, anyway. Nicky wants his mother, and more than likely you do too."

But Mona was not coming home for Christmas, he said.

Brad thawed fish-sticks in the microwave, poured Allegra another glass of wine. He attempted to explain.

"Her parents are in Florida for the winter," he said. "Now that her dad's retired they go there every year, join the snow geese or whatever they are called."

"Birds, I think."

Allegra was succumbing thankfully to the warmth and the smell of frying food and the wine. All those Canadians flying south, dangling their suitcases and their golf bags, honking, changing leaders from time to time. No doubt down in Florida the residents looked up from their green lawns and shopping plazas and remarked on the change of season when they spotted the first flight.

"So this year, with Mona already in the east, her mother went ahead and made arrangements for her and Nicky, and me, to go. She did all this before I knew anything about it, rented another unit next to theirs. Then she told Nicky on the phone, before I had a chance to say no." He was explaining all this while he gave the fish sticks elaborate attention. "So now Nicky is so excited that of course I can't let him down."

"No of course you can't let him down."

Two units, side by side—one for the parents and one for...whom? Nicky and Brad? And in the other one with the parents, Mona on the couch? Unlikely scene.

But who could be heartless enough to want to deny a little boy his mother, at Christmas? "I think you are a wonderful father," was all she whispered, much later. into the crevice between his adams apple and his chin.

Being with a man had so little to do with words, and little to do with touching, really, either. It had more to do with lying still and passing something back and forth through joined surfaces of skin. That was why you had to sleep with a man, literally sleep, in the same house, night after night.

§

Now Arachne, the daughter of a dyer of Phocaean purple, rose above herself. She was a beautiful girl, extravagant of dress. But her great claim to fame was her weaving skill.

We are told that the nymphs would leave their woods and vineyards and golden streams to come and watch her as she wound the rough skeins of wool into balls or smoothed it, drawing the fleece into threads, twisting the spindle with her clever thumb, adding sparks of embroidery. People began to say that she must have been taught by Athena herself. When Arachne heard this, she was offended.

"Let her come and weave against me then," she said, "and we will see who can teach something to the other!"

Athena came to her in the guise of an old woman, and suggested that such a duel would not be wise. Arachne scorned this, saying that if Athena would not accept the challenge she must be afraid she would not win. Athena suddenly appeared before the girl as herself.

The nymphs bowed down. But Arachne repeated her challenge, and this time Athena, furious, accepted.

"At once they both set up their looms and stretched out on them the delicate warp. The web was fastened to the beam," Ovid tells us, giving details of early weaving techniques, "reeds separated the threads and through the threads went the sharp shuttles which their fingers sped. Quickly they worked, with their clothes tucked up round their breasts, their skilled hands moving backwards and forwards like lightning...they used all the colours that are made by the merchants of Tyre, the purple of the oyster and every other dye, each shading into each...as after a storm of rain, when a rainbow spans the sky...and in their work they wove in stiff threads of gold, telling ancient stories."

Think of all the things Arachne could have woven into her design that might have spared her the worst of Athena's wrath. How the goddess had saved her city from a volcanic eruption long before, or how she joined her father Zeus in leading the gods in their victorious conflict with the giants— how she struck a rock with her sword and there sprang up the olive tree. Athena was used to being celebrated. Every year two young girls were chosen to weave a cloth that told all manner of her triumphs, and this cloth was then ceremonially draped upon the statue of the goddess that stood in the Acropolis. Instead Arachne wove stories of the many scandalous love affairs among the gods. Athena wove stern moral tales of mortals who tried to rise too high.

We have a reminder of how the tale of Arachne ends every time we swipe away a spider web.

§

The night before Brad and Nicky went off to Florida, Allegra celebrated an early Christmas with them at her apartment. She had brought in a feast from a deli up on Davie Street, Cornish game hens and wild rice pilaf and a pudding she got Brad to flambé. She gave Nicky a book about explorers. She gave Brad a set of artist quality oils, because the ones he'd been using were running low. He handed her a package that she knew would be perfume. How did he know which one to buy?

The green-and-white-striped bottle was familiar. *Ma Griffe*. She'd seen the abandoned dregs of the same perfume at the back of the bathroom cupboard he and Mona used to share.

Before leaving home next day she had put on her Russian fur, her tall red hat. She caught her reflection in the window of a shelter for the homeless down on Hastings Street. An outlandish furry creature rolling along like a circus bear.

When she got to the studio no one was there. The place was open, all the dyes in bottles gleaming on the shelves like jewels. Had they all been overcome by the festive spirit and gone off for drinks leaving the door unlocked?

Then suddenly, they all came bursting out of the office. There had just been a call from Customs. The silk had arrived, the whole two hundred thousand yards. Even their broker didn't seem to know the story, whether it was the first shipment or the replacement. Five hundred bales! It would be a big operation just to take possession of it, but Allegra could not stand to delay one more day. She had already arranged storage in a nearby warehouse. Now Jim managed to get hold of a five-ton delivery truck, with a dolly and a couple of men who agreed to work late to get the whole lot shifted. The whole crew went along to help. "Bring enough back here for us to get going," Allegra said. She waited at the studio with Faye.

"Let's set up the screens for the first colour-way on the lily design. We can start printing right away."

ᵹᴑ

Manny and Jim staggered in carrying bales. The fabric was baled in plastic, underneath wrapped in heavy paper that had the smell of jasmine— or frankincense, or myrrh— a smell of mystery and promise. The silk lifted, sighed, gave off its complicated breath, as they cut the string. Fine heavy silk twill, exactly what they had ordered, suitable for the most expensive fashions.

When Asia and the crew came back from the warehouse, they had picked up a jug of Lesser Okanagan. Jim poured them all a tumbler of wine.

"Keep back from the silk," Allegra said. She could see they were not going to get any more work done that night.

"No, I'm fine," she told Jim, when everyone went home. "I just want to stay here and breathe in the smell of the silk for a while."

She started rifling through her bag for her address book. Brad didn't know she'd gone through his desk and come across the address in Florida, where Mona's parents were staying. He wouldn't be there yet. But she could leave him a message.

Eventually she managed to get Information to track down the

phone number that went with the address. A woman with a sweet but not entirely sober voice answered the phone.

"Oh dear," she said. "Oh dear, no you've got it wrong. They won't be here tonight. They are all stopping in Orlando. Are you a friend of Mona's? Yes, Mona's stopping there too. Disneyland. Just a couple of days, then they're all coming down."

§

She called a cab. She put her coat on, and her hat. She locked the shop and went out onto the street to await the humiliation involved in taking one of those wheelchair equipped taxis: of teetering dangerously up the narrow ramp, strapped down like a piece of furniture.

She gave the driver Brad's address.

§

Others who famously dressed above their station include Pandora, who though she was girdled by Athena did not put on her wise restraint.

And Agrippina, mother of Nero, who is said to have owned a robe made entirely of spun gold. This was Caligula's sister. She secured the throne for her son by intelligent use of poison, and in return he extended the cup to her.

And Niobe, queen of Thebes.

Like Arachne, Niobe scorned the gods. When the Theban women filled the temple to worship the goddess Leto, "Suddenly, in a swirl of attendants, Niobe was among them...like a great flame, in her robes of golden tissue," scouring the worshippers with a look of scorn, then turning her rage on the goddess for accepting the tribute Niobe thought was owed to her. This did not work

December

in Niobe's favour. Once her entire family had been slain in retribution, "Her open eyes became stones. Her whole body a stone...Her tongue solidified in her stone mouth." On a mountain top somewhere in Greece that stone is weeping still.

How deep in our bones is this awareness. It avails little to wrap up in swirls of golden tissue—to imagine you are central to the tale.

℘

Allegra's hands shook terribly as she unlocked the front door. She nearly dropped the key. Suppose Brad's flight had been cancelled, or made to detour, or been hijacked—suppose he suddenly arrived back—suppose he'd gone as far as Seattle and changed his mind, and decided that the only thing he wanted to do at Christmas was spend it with her?

When she finally managed to get in, her eye fell on the wicker trunk. Today it wasn't even locked. The box was merely held shut with a wooden peg through the clasp.

℘

The trunk was not full of photographs or albums or old clippings, or family things of any sort. It was full of drawings.

These were not the highlights of her life that he had allowed her to see. These were drawings of her body in its sickness, in its slackness, in tiredness or pain. These were drawings of her self—powerful, terrible. She wanted to gather the whole lot and throw them in the fireplace. If the chimney didn't work, if the house filled with smoke, if all his other pictures were destroyed, if the fire engines came and the entire contents of the house got water-logged, he would know that everybody has their limit. She was weak with anger, sick with shame.

She tore a whole sheaf of drawings out of the chest. Suddenly, she glimpsed the face of Mona staring up at her. Page after page of Mona's clear scythe-like features, her hair sometimes curving around her face like red-brown polished wood, an odd contrast to the black line of her brows as they pulled together in a frown. Or Mona, leaning forward, her elbows on her knees, her hair strangely shorn and ragged, as if just that morning she had hacked it off with garden shears. She was wearing black jeans and a white t-shirt and jogging shoes, a geometric figure of fierce and utter concentration, made the more striking by the wild shorn hair that shone like broken amber glass. Allegra reached further into the pile.

Then she dropped the sketches, shoved everything back in and slammed the lid. She rammed the stick into the latch. She had seen cut-off arms and legs and quartered torsos, face-down heads streaming hair. Body parts both male and female, small neat sketches covering just one crumpled sheet that had been straightened out again. Bodies cut apart with precise butchery, yet the muscles tensed, as if caught alive, ready to jump right off the page.

But this was an anatomy lesson, surely.

She began to understand that the drawings of herself were what had really shaken her. The attention to disintegration. Of course it wasn't fair to judge something that was never intended to be seen.

$\wp$

She sank back inside another taxi, that hump-backed shell, and let bad feeling rise like bile. The moving shoppers on the street were flat as paving stones, flat as the outlines of shot bodies, sprawled face down, moving along a conveyor belt.

"Just pull off onto the second ramp, when we get across the bridge," she told the driver. "I'll direct you from there. I live down on Pacific. I want to go straight home."

She was very conscious of all the lights, as the car arced across the bridge: hundreds of twinkling arrangements spelling out reproof beamed at her from the stars on top of buildings, the strings of lights on apartment balconies, the towering construction cranes.

Her driver was heading straight down Granville Mall when he should have turned.

"Never mind giving me the damn scenic tour—just turn up Davie, I live over on Pacific!" East Indian music was twining loudly from the speakers. He couldn't hear. She leaned forward to tap him on the shoulder, but she couldn't reach him, and they were floating up toward Georgia, past the brilliant windows and the crowds of people heading to a concert at the Orpheum. He kept going right up to Robson, where he decided to make a left-hand turn.

"Stop!" she shouted suddenly. "Stop, stop, STOP!" There, someone on the corner. A young woman standing on the pavement, who—despite the pale hair, the elegance, the smart grey hooded cape, the boots which in the street lights had a buttery gleam—despite all the obvious differences of costume, looked so like Allegra.

Now the driver sensed her panic, and he unstrapped her, helped her down the wobbly ramp. Still, by the time she got out onto the street the young woman in the grey cape had crossed at the light. Allegra called after her. "ANGELINE!"

Allegra ripped across Robson against the light. She knew it was her daughter. That beautiful young woman with the swinging stride. Her daughter. Exactly as she had always pictured her. Allegra zigzagged through the crowds. She thought she caught a glimpse of the cape disappearing in the crowd across the street. At the Orpheum, she became tangled up again in the throng of people streaming in. The Vancouver Symphony, the Bach Magnificat.

She pushed up to the booth. Amazingly they had a ticket, even though she would require a special seat at the back of the lower balcony. She made her way around to the side entrance and up the elevator. She wouldn't be able to wander the lobbies. The orchestra was tuning up. The choir came in, young men in dinner jackets, the women in taffeta dresses of black, or red, or electric blue. She had not been to a concert here for so long. Her eyes wandered over the old theatre, taking in the mural on the ceiling, the ornate cream-and-gilded pillars carved with intricate patterns.

The first violin strode in. The orchestra came to order. The conductor— Maestro Akiyama, silver-haired and slim, his aquiline face beaming— walked lightly to the podium and bowed. He turned, raised his baton. In the hush that followed, the choir rose.

January

*U*ntil the middle ages, most cloth was woven in the home. If a family had excess, it would be sold to the feudal lord as part payment of taxes—and the Lord of the Manor then marked it with his personal brand. The brand became known as a product's guarantee of quality.

This branded cloth was sold at huge annual European fairs that attracted merchants from all over the civilized world. Such fairs were held as early as the time of Charlemagne, but the trade in cloth itself is older still. Linen was a recognized form of currency of ancient Egypt. The Phoenicians came as far as Britain to trade purple cloth for tin. Assyrian traders on the well-established route to Anatolia wrote letters home in cuneiform, telling their wives to get busy weaving themselves, to send more goods along as fast as possible by mule.

When the secrets of silk reached Italy at last, the walled city of Lucca began producing brocades such as have never been seen before or since. Such surreal patterns, such fantasy. Flying snakes, boating dogs, winged leopards—faces growing from the roots of trees— but most significant, the way glittering rays of light streamed from the motifs, as if struck with other-worldly fire....

℘

Allegra held off until the second weekend after Brad got home before returning to his house.

He had come to see her, almost as soon as he got back. He brought her the perfect gift, a small silver soap dish, with a cover in elaborate filigree.

"It must have cost the earth."

"Open it."

The monogrammed letters on the lid were very fine and spidery. She couldn't make them out.

"I love antiques. I love the sense of touching other lives without ever knowing who they belonged to." Brad was wearing a new plaid flannel shirt, expensive, soft. Inside the silver box was a sea horse on a bed of purple, a little creature white as bone, the long flared snout, the curled-under tail.

"This is beautiful." She tried to concentrate on what she knew. "I heard something about sea horses once. I think it was that when they mate they produce musical sounds. Imagine the deeps of the sea echoing with the sound of them chasing one-another in circles, like tiny carousels." She had things more important to tell him, but she decided to wait.

"Did it come like this, in this beautiful box? Someone's treasure?"

"Yes."

That had been the extent of their conversation about his trip.

℘

January

Nicky had a cold, so the three of them were spending the day inside, Brad completely absorbed, Nicky restive and petulant, the windows to the street obscured by elaborate patterns of frost. If she had known that Nicky was sick, she wouldn't have come.

On every side were subjects better left unbroached. Night after night, during Brad's absence, she had vowed not to say a word about the drawings in the chest, but instead to tell him about a revelation. She had worked on her tapestry for Angeline, feeling so resolved since that night at the Orpheum that even beneath her slow fingers the flame pattern had flared up around the small dark lump, like a knob of coal, which would soon be consumed by the brilliance of her knotted strands. Surely, now, she was not going to sink back into their Saturday routine without saying anything at all, when ever since that night at the Orpheum she had been burning to tell him what she had learned. Brad, I found myself at that concert almost by chance, following a phantom, a figure in a cape.

She had to make him understand what had happened when the choir rose that night, when the music rose in her heart. On that darkest night of the year the same thing was happening all around the earth, voices were curling up from this singular sprouting planet into the black of space, and she knew that her daughter was somewhere in the world, and that she could bear it if she never saw her, for Angeline had brought her to that moment when her heart, which had been so clenched and tight and scared, could quietly uncurl.

She understood now that love was very large. It was okay for him to love Mona, he ought to love Mona, he could love Mona without ever having to fear what she, Allegra, might think or say.

And she understood his need to paint in any way he chose. For in that moment at the Orpheum she had also had an extraordinary sense of herself. If she could hold onto that, she was immune.

℘

She and Nicky were supposed to be playing Scrabble, but he'd become frustrated and messed up the board. Brad was working on a painting of something she wished she had never told him about.

In this painting the torn edges of the hooked rug made a rhythmic pattern as the threads tangled and curled back upon themselves. Deep inside, in a circle of light, Allegra was on top of the small mountain in the Okanagan, spreading her wide white sleeves. Everything was there, the lake broken up in waves, the pine-dotted hills, the north wind lifting her flowing hair, all portrayed with the exacting brush-strokes of a Persian miniature.

Nicky had moved the Scrabble box over to the top of the wicker chest. He was building a railroad with the word-shelves laid out like the tracks, the ridges of the wicker holding them up like trestles. He pushed the letters along these in a line.

Allegra had brought along the proofs of photos of their work she had taken, which would go with the ads coming out later in the spring.

Nicky carried in a glass of apple juice. He had it teetering on the chest beside his train. Allegra hoped the juice would spill.

She wheeled herself over to the front window. The panes were like small frosted scenes, each capturing a dipping, rearing land where feathery ferns grew out of dense, crystal ground. In some places the plumes had grown above the others to a height of an inch or two, and these sent roots deep into the sparkling earth, thrusting to the bottom of the pane. Here and there above all this, in the clear glass air, were a few loose crystals, some like falling leaves, some like flocks of winter birds with tiny outstretched wings.

She felt herself stiffen. How these scenes paralleled Brad's tiny paintings; he had her trapped like a fly in amber. On and on with this he went, using up their nights, using up their days, nothing ever coming to anything between them while he went on creating artificial worlds, refusing to show his work to anyone. And in his damn box the brilliant drawings of her flapped and groaned. She wasted vital energy rooting them out like weeds whenever they cropped up in her head, for now the flowers of Patience, Goodness, Compliance, Discipline, the garden of letting well enough alone thrived, where she breathed the druggy thought that surely his strength would grow around her need as naturally as the roots of a tree might grow around some burden in the soil.

She pushed herself away from the window and into the kitchen, so fast that her wheel took a chunk of paint off the door.

She had done all this before, gathered up her things, determined never to come again. She was transferring her gear from the kitchen table to her Mexican bag, when there was a pounding at the door.

"Will somebody get that?" Brad called.

In the other room, Nicky kept on with his game. The banging began again, insistent, rhythmic.

"Nicky, will you please get the door!"

Not long ago there had been a home invasion just blocks away, the same set of circumstances, a child answering the door and then a bunch of hooded thugs bursting in. Allegra pushed back into the living room, just as Nicky took off the latch.

The door burst open. A man leapt into the room with a

dancer's stride, at the same moment removing his tall black hat so that a flock of doves flew out. The birds circled the room, ruffling the air with their wings; the whole place started to spin, the room whirled like a merry-go-round. Nicky jumped up on Allegra's lap. The man held up his hat again, and the birds flew in and disappeared. Silence, save for the soft music of their cooing.

He was in white-face, dressed in black, a mime. For the next half hour he found flowers growing in the folds of the curtains, plucked an egg from Nicky's ear, pulled a large pink-eyed rabbit from his hat, did conjuring tricks with red handkerchiefs and fans and finished with another sweep of his hat which filled the room with butterflies. Later Allegra and Nicky both swore they had felt the brush of wings. Then as suddenly as this magician had appeared, he was gone.

"Dad, you knew him, didn't you?"

A smile and a shrug.

"Where did he come from, if you didn't know him?"

"Sometimes nice things happen for no reason, I guess." He came and put his arm around Allegra.

"That was so incredible, so lovely," she said later while he was washing up the dinner dishes, and she—at knee-height—was scraping leftovers into the garbage.

Getting to understand a man was like traveling in a foreign country: you landed, and it was all steel drums and swaying palms, and the longer you stayed the less you knew.

His hands were still hot and soapy, but he took hers and looked at them for a long moment before he bent down and lifted her so she was standing, leaning up against the sink. Wetness from his hands seeped through her blouse. He still didn't say anything, but he touched her so she felt a stirring like that swarm of butterflies.

She said, "I don't think I should go home tonight."

§

In his bedroom there was nothing to make you think of Mona, no scent, no photographs, no clothes. Mona's presence had been erased so completely that it gathered strength out of the unfresh smell of the sheets, the lumpy pillows, the way the bedroom curtain had come unhooked, letting in light from the street.

Brad didn't touch her. She lay awake for hours, conscious of all the unfamiliar sounds, the clanking of the radiator pipes, the rumble of the fridge, the unexplainable creaking of floor-boards from the attic room above, until finally her thoughts became one with the mottled darkness of the room. She was dreaming a long many-chambered dream, moving through sweetness; the rooms and the adventures changed, but she was running through a honey-textured light. She woke to brilliant sunlight, and little Nicky's stare.

February

There have always been sound reasons for society's strictures. In Italy the cost of a daughter's trousseau became so extreme that fathers dreaded the birth of a girl. At the same time women had become so expensive of dress that young men had qualms about taking wives. The devil was at the door. Soon the merest wardrobe of a lady of position—like that of Mona Margherita Datani, wife of a merchant of Prato, whose dresses included a gown of purple lined with green, and another of blue damask trimmed with ermine, and a cloak lined with pale blue taffeta, and a modest ash-coloured robe with a border of miniver at the hem—such obvious essentials were "the fruit of robbery and usury," San Bernardino preached, "of peasants' sweat and widows' blood, of the very marrow of unprotected orphans. If you were to take one of these gowns and press it and wring it out, you would see, gushing out of it, a human being's blood!"

Yet sumptuary laws have never managed to suppress the desire for adornment, but rather have served to spur the invention of extravagance.

§

The Halcyon dyes were selling themselves. The brilliance of the colour, and the ease of application (water-based; no solvents needed to clean up the squeegees and the screens) made them attractive both to commercial printers of towels and bags and t-shirts, and for use in homes and schools. They could be used right on the kitchen counter, if you discounted the matter of the noxious curing fumes. And buyers seemed to be attracted to the promise of the calm and quietude of their namesake.

Such a flurry of activity in the decrepit building on Cordova Street during that period not too long past the winter solstice, as Faye and Asia laboured at the long printing table, day after day, stretching out the lengths of shimmering white silk, pinning it down onto the back-cloth, then precisely aligning all the clamps at designated spots, to hold the screens. The screens stretched the width of the table, and when the printing began Faye would stand at one side, Asia at the other, and push the squeegee back and forth to make one print, then the next.

Allegra, while the preparation work was going on, ran the final colour checks. Then the dye was mixed in large buckets, which had to match the samples they had sent.

Jim had been at work on publicity. One day—just when they were in full production—a reporter from Habitat arrived. A slim man with lemon-coloured hair. He wore wrap-around dark glasses he never removed. There was a photographer too, a gruff fellow in a lumberjack shirt. The journalist's name was Flyte. She wasn't sure if this was his first name or his last. Flyte had trouble grasping the concept of what silk-screen printing *was*.

"Look, here," she said, "you're just in time to see us start a run of colour. This is the first screen we're going to use. It's just like a window screen really, only with a tightly-stretched mesh of nylon instead of wire. And the nylon is covered with a tough impermeable layer, except—Jim, could you hold this up to the light?—except for the open spaces, where the dye will be pushed through. See how on this one the openings are narrow oblongs with a wavy s-shape at either end? Like joints of bamboo? That's because we're about to print stripes. Then over that we're putting flowers." He didn't take a note. The photographer was shuffling through the rack that held the rest of the screens for this design.

"Are these photo-screens?"

"Yes we shoot our delicate ones with photographic positives."

"Excellent detail."

"The leaf skeletons? Yes, aren't they pretty. We've designed it to create a lace pattern. But on this one..." she turned back to Flyte, "we're going to start by printing continuous stripes, as I said. A real tour-de-force."

"Does this stuff stain?" Flyte said.

"Maybe you should take your nice jacket off. Here I'll give you an apron."

They stood and watched as Faye and Asia set the first screen in place on the registration bar. "We make all our screens the same size," Allegra said. "And all our designs are based on an eighteen-inch repeat, so that we never have to change the system, whatever design; we just move whatever screen we're using from hinge to hinge, and it all works out."

Faye poured dye onto the wide area on her side of the screen where there was no opening at all. She took her fat rubber squeegee in two hands. With steady pressure she pushed the jellied-looking dye-paste across the table to where Asia had her hands stretched to grasp the wooden handle and pull the colour (deep gold) the rest of the way. They passed the squeegee back and forth like this, with the screen in the same position, several times. Then Faye scraped what dye remained into a thin obedient line in the dye-well ("That's the covered area of the screen at this end," Allegra explained), took the pins from the hinges, lifted the screen. Underneath, across the width of the silk, were seven wavy oblongs of varied widths, all eighteen inches long, with what looked like bites taken out of them along the sides.

"In a continuous pattern, every second image has to be printed, all the way down the table," Allegra was explaining, "because as you can see the screen is much wider than the print it makes. Then we come back and fill in the spaces in between. Otherwise the screen would pick up wet dye on its underside, and this would smear." The printers set the screen down and made the second print and picked it up again.

"But those don't join up," Flye said. "I thought you said you were making stripes."

"That will happen. Believe me, the stripes will magically appear. You have to be patient. Write that down. This is a long and tedious process, worth every penny the product costs when it's done."

While the printers were working their way down the table doing the first segments of the stripes, Flyte pulled out his phone and went off into the office to make some calls.

"Now look," Allegra said, calling him back eventually, "while they've been moving down the table Jim has been moving this fan behind them." She pointed to the big electric fan that ran on a wire track above the table. As far as she knew, the way it had been rigged up to glide along was their own invention. "So now the dye is dry, we can begin filling in."

Sure enough, as they moved back up the table a continuous stripe began to appear, the wavy ends interlocking so that if there happened to be the smallest overlap, or gap, the eye filled it in. "That is part of the hand-printed effect. The tiny irregularities that let you know you've got a hand-made product. People pay extra for the artistic errors we occasionally make. Don't write that."

The photographer was shaking his head. "A long and arduous process. What comes next?"

"Well, we print one colour this way, and then there is a new screen for the next. You see where those stripes are indented? That's where the purple clematis are going to appear. There will be a screen for the petals, and then one for the small green bristly pistils, and then we'll do the dark outlines of the leaves and stems, which will twine all the way up and also carry the eye along.

"And all this has to be planned beforehand," she said, getting carried away, "because also each colour when it overlaps another will blend to make a still new and different colour. Just think," she was determined to get some reaction from Flyte, "what intelligence is at work here," she gestured towards her helpers, "to create these yards of riches, to bring to life such a play of patterning and colours. And it's all conjured from a white slate! Magic!"

"So this is going to be used for fashion?" Flyte said.

"Yes, you came on one of our fashion days," she said airily. "But of course we also do custom printing for interior design."

She had no idea what he would make of this, but the photo-grapher had taken dozens of shots. The article would be out in about six months, Flye said, as he slid carefully into his jacket and out to his rented Porsche.

Then he was back. "What would it cost to get a shirt made out of that?" indicating the design that was growing on the table.

"Well," Allegra said. "as luck would have it we have some sample yardage, right here. It has just one small flaw. But then as I was saying, this can also be a virtue. The Japanese for example—with their tea-bowls, made by potters who are national treasures—always make sure to avoid complete perfection, which is regarded as insulting to the gods. Here I'll tell you what. I'll give you the name of a wonderful seamstress. If you go along right now, I'm sure she will make it up for you. No no. It's on the house."

<p>

In the Kyoto of the Lady Murasaki (who wrote about the royal court at the end of the first millennium) the costume of the noble ladies was a garment called the junihitoe, made with between twelve and twenty robes of silk, worn one above the next. A narrow band of each overlapping garment was visible at the neck and sleeves and hem. Great importance was put upon the colour combinations of these over-lapping layers.

In the Edo period the samurai class was often hopelessly in debt because of the huge amounts they spent on what they wore. This led to a royal edict against the wearing of silk. Rich merchants turned to the dyers for new ideas. Hence the yukata, a simple unlined cotton garment first worn in the bath houses. This became a complexly stenciled garment in many shades of indigo.

In the twelfth century, the samurai class took control. They too placed restrictions on dress, choosing the practical garb of commoners for themselves—better to wear in battle, and more in line with the simplicity of warrior life. The women also stripped away their many layers, adopting just the kosode, which had previously been the undergarment of the bulky junihitoe. From this the kimono grew, a practical garment, which closed only with a sash. The plainness of this garment was relieved by new and elaborate dye techniques, for example shibori (tie-dye) and the application of printed gold and silver leaf (surihaku). The tying of the sash became an art form all its own.

In the fourteenth century, the Ashikaga family came to power, avid patrons of the arts: this is known as the Muromachi period. The wealthy merchants wanted more and more elaborate textiles, and among other things tsujigahana (stitched tie-dye combined with ink painting, gold and silver leaf, and embroidery on silk) began to evolve. It was during the following Momoyama period that this art reached its peak, allowing the creation of some of the most glorious kimonos ever made, before the technique fell victim to its own complexity.

§

The New York job was nearly done. Just one final bolt to print. All the rest had been cured and safely folded, wrapped in golden tissue ready to send off. The project had garnered much excitement around the city. After a glowing article in the weekend paper, FibreWorks had become almost public property, people feeling free to drop by.

These last weeks, her crew had been here around the clock, Faye and Asia and three students taking turns with the printing, Jim moving the drying fans then running the silk through the curing machine, Manny doing all the heavy work. Allegra felt lazy compared to the rest of them. She was physically much weaker lately, sometimes unable to work the controls of her chair. She didn't want to think about what might be making her feel so shaky. The excitement of the project kept her going.

As usual, that day they printed the background first (the blotch) a midnight blue. Once printed it left a ghost of the coming design, like a photograph in negative, indicating half-formed in white the petals, stems, leaves. Then screen by screen the pattern took on definition, colour. By the time it was finished, it was late afternoon.

Jim went to the big old fridge at the back, which contained mainly pots of dye, and produced a bottle of champagne. When the phone started ringing, they all ignored it and raised their glassed in a toast.

The phone rang at least ten times, then stopped, then rang again. "Okay, okay, okay," Jim finally said as he went to answer it.

"Well but did you cure them?" Allegra could hear his careful level voice, as she made her way through into the office. He was hunched over the old roll-top desk, peering right and left beneath his bushy eyebrows as he took notes on a pad.

What began as one ill-timed phone call, soon became a flood. That afternoon it was a near-hysterical printer of motel towels. "Did you do tests before you sent your order off?" Jim was asking. The printer had gone swimming in the pool of the building where he lived, taking with him a towel left over from a recent order printed with their dyes. The towel had fallen into the water. The water had turned green. The man had stood watching as the pattern lifted and floated away. "If you read the instructions again, you will see that tests are essential," Jim was explaining evenly.

They continued to field these frantic calls—to explain the same thing over and over—for the next few weeks. They were always extremely helpful and sympathetic.

At first Allegra kept praying that this was a problem of their customers' negligence and haste. She ran some further tests on the New York order, hesitating to send it off. She cut off strips and sent them out to be cleaned. She ran the bolts through the curing machine again and tested them. She could not get the dye to withstand the tests, even when she cranked up the heat of the machine to the point where the fabric scorched.

"I just do not understand what went wrong," she said to Brad, when she finally had to admit that it was an out-and-out disaster. Jim had called Brad to come down to the studio. She was having a spell.

"Look, how do you know that it's not just a matter of time," Brad said.

"What do you mean?"

"Perhaps the dye will settle in, in time. Think how long it will take, before the fabric is even made into clothes. It could be a couple of years before any of those garments are sent out to be cleaned."

"What are you suggesting? That I send the fabric off, and take the money?"

"It's a chance to get your finances straightened out."

"And wait to get sued?"

He couldn't be paying attention to what she was saying. "I can't believe what I'm hearing." She began churning her wheel chair up and down the room, desperate strength flooding back. He turned pale. She felt strong enough to tear him to shreds. "I can't believe I am living through the most disastrous crisis of my life, and all you want to do is hush it up, so you can go home and go on painting your little saccharine scenes. And all the while, you are hiding the real stuff, aren't you?

"What?"

"In your damn wicker box."

He turned and walked out. She heard the tinkle of the shop bell. The clang of the door.

℘

When Allegra refused to send off the doubtful yardage, Faye tried to persuade her to look into renting the space and the equipment to start a professional textile school. People would come from all over the country, Faye assured her, to use the set-up they had. Then Allegra had two unexpected breaks. A set designer for a movie dropped by, looking for several hundred yards of exotic fabric to drape the atrium of the courthouse, where they planned to shoot a dreamlike circus scene. So she was able to sell off the printed silk at something close to cost. The plain silk Jim would be able to wholesale, gradually. The rest of the printing equipment—table, screens and dyes—she unloaded on a man who turned up looking for advice, hoping to set up a print shop on a communal farm in the Kootenays.

"It's a tricky business," Allegra told him. "I have to warn you that we have had some problems with these dyes. You'll need to run a lot of tests. It could take a while to get it right. You better get in touch with the manufacturer in Germany." The farmer said they were growing some lucrative alternate crops, so he was not in a hurry, but they needed to diversify, "If you know what I mean."

Like Pompeii, her entire culture had been buried beneath the ash, and she kept trying to dig back down and re-inhabit it. She tried to locate the moment when she could have stepped in and turned everything around.

<p>

She had not seen Brad since that day. She hadn't left the apartment. She was afraid to use the phone, in case it was tied up when he called.

Now, one more day, she looked around at all the reflections of herself, against a rain-filled, mirrored sky. And suddenly light was streaming down all the mirrors, and the watery reflections were brimming silver, and she was remembering how she had stood on top of a mountain long ago, before she let a lot of people tell her what she could and couldn't do. That came first, and quickly faded. What remained in the hollow of that light was an idea so obvious she could not imagine why it had never come to her before.

March

When we consider innovations in the art of weaving, we might study the technique devised by the Lady Nabeshima, who——needing something to fill her idle hours——began to ply gold and silver threads into the traditional patterns of Japan, as in the well known Ocean Wave. Famous also is the gossamer known as Tsuzure Ori, a technique where the weaver's fingernails were filed into sharp serrated points and used in turn, so that by the time the last nail had worn down, the first had re-grown.

Whatever the technique, Repetition and Variation remain key. Here we pluck the uneasy thread that runs through design and myth in every land: the suspicion that things are not what they seem.

A parallel theme——another stripe if you will——is that of the surprise *that lies in wait (think of Arachne; think of poor Actaeon who merely looked at a goddess bathing in a stream) for those who reach for more than they deserve.*

In Corinth there was a king—a great horseman—who fed his horses human flesh to make them fierce. He was thrown from his chariot and torn to pieces by his steeds, devoured. He might have expected something of the sort. Less predictable was the fate of the boy who many claimed was his son, the young hero Bellerophon.

ᆼ

From the moment Brad first paused over the stack of drawing paper and picked up one of Mona's 3-B pencils, it was like a childhood dream: he could fly.

Strange as this had been, this unexpected talent laying a hand on him, the attraction to Allegra had been even stranger. Again and again, just as on that day when he had stood among the wreckage of the glass house in the Properties and felt the sadness and the terror and the waste flashing from all those broken panes, there were moments in his life when he felt the centre drop away. Then, as if the very plunge had cracked open an entirely new dimension, he would have to see her. Yet even the first time he breathed on her skin and felt the shiver of her striving so hard to feel, his sight of her had been distanced, narrowed. He felt the peculiar tension of her plight. I must record this, was what snaked into his head.

Night after night Brad's unexpected talent was there, was everything.

And then it was gone.

ᆼ

Some said the youth Bellerophon was the son of the king; others whispered that Poseidon was his father. Whatever the truth, the young man dreamed of horses too.

He learned of the winged steed Pegasus, wild, untamable, who roamed the skies. He knew he had no hope of catching such a horse. Still, he pined. At last a wise old man advised him to go to the temple of Athena and sleep in that sacred place. And there Bellerophon had a dream that the goddess was standing before him holding a bridle of gold. He sprang awake. The goddess was gone, but the bridle remained. That is how he charmed the winged horse. He found the beautiful Pegasus grazing in a field and when he approached, the horse whinnied and trotted towards him and allowed the golden bit to be slipped into its mouth.

℘

The way Allegra had acted that day in the studio, like a wild woman, her hair flying. Then worse, the revelation that she had leafed through all the things in the wicker chest, seen drawings that had been torn from him in the dark hours of the night when his hand was not his own. In those, he believed he had stretched out the lineaments of her pain into an almost sensuous thing. But she had seen the other drawing too, which on the worst nights forced their way onto the page. Sometimes he thought those drawings came from the fire at the centre of the world. He had no idea what he himself might be capable of, if the circumstances of his safe life changed, if the fire caught him.

℘

After capturing Pegasus, Bellerophon got into trouble, as people often do when their dreams are fulfilled. No one remembers how this happened, but he killed his brother. To be shriven of this dreadful deed he went to Argos where the king purified him and accepted him as a guest. The king's wife fell in love with him, there, and when he would have nothing to do with her she told the king that he had assaulted her and must die. The king could not bring himself to offend against the ancient laws of hospitality, so he contrived a scheme that resulted in the young man being sent off to fight the Chimera, a beast part lion, part goat, with a serpent's tail and a breath of flame. This monster, unassailable by land, was easily approached from the sky. Bellerophon flew over him on Pegasus and rained arrows into the creature's heart.

The hero went on to perform many other feats that would have been impossible for an earth-bound man. For a long time he lived happily, but at last he forgot that his success had all been due to a gift from the gods. He decided that he deserved to become a god himself. He tried to ride his winged steed straight up to Olympus.

Pegasus was wiser. He threw his former master to the earth. Bellerophon, "hated of the gods" wandered alone from that time on, "devouring his own soul and avoiding the paths of men until he died."

§

When Brad returned to his nightly sketching he felt claustrophobic. He could still move his pencil with the same fluidity, but he felt greyness and guilt and extreme unease.

Even after he went back to Allegra this carried on, though he forced himself to sit down each night and draw.

If he could have said, "I had a gift but it has left me," it would have been easier to accept. But what Brad saw—as he sat in his kitchen one night while the rain fell and a moth kept banging round and round within the Chinese paper globe so that a fine dusty precipitation fell inside as well—was that he had never had anything more than a certain point of view. He recalled a story from his childhood. He saw a grey man in a cave, stooped and cold. The man sat with sacks of coins spilling all around, and chests of treasure: star-sapphires, and ropes of honey-coloured diamonds, and rubies bleeding onto the glitter that all the gold coins gave. And the man remembered exactly how he had acquired all these things, and how he had felt the day before, and he picked up a handful from the chest before him so his hands were stained with gobs of thrilling light, and he thought: stones.

℘

It was midnight, or after. When the phone rang, for once it was a relief. Brad knew it would be Allegra. He had told her he would drop by.

"Oh, you're there! I guess it's kind of late for me to call, but I thought you said...."

"No," Brad said, "it's fine."

"What's going on? You sound strange."

"An amazing thing just happened."

"Really?"

He wished he was with her, could bury his face in her hair, let what felt like years of striving trickle away.

"I seem to have quit," he said.

"Well...that's good news. Now you'll have more time to paint."

"But that's what I've quit."

"I don't understand."

"I've quit painting, Allegra. I don't know what happened. It's not there anymore. Maybe it never was."

"I don't know what to say. Only, listen, I was hoping you'd come over tonight. I had a wonderful surprise, but of course it won't mean anything now."

"What do you mean? Why not?"

"The thing is, I've just managed to get you a show"

Now he recalled the last time he'd seen her in her apartment, surrounded by photographic gear.

"I've decided to start making a record of your work," she'd said, as if nothing had come between them at the studio, though her face was pale, her skin looked parched. "How did you think we'd managed the pictures for the ads? I even took pictures for a paper once when I lived up north."

When he'd brought her to his place with all her photographic paraphernalia he'd decided this was just another of her whims, but he had set up her tripod where she asked, and directed the lights where she wanted. He had had no idea she would take a portfolio of these slides around to all the galleries she approved of, going back several times if necessary. She'd done it all in secret, for fear he would disapprove.

And as a result, the DeVere had actually offered him a show. That was what she was telling him as he stood there worrying at the knots in the phone cord.

"Of course Erica DeVere needs to come and meet you", Allegra said. "Erica needs to see the actual work. But it is a ninety-nine percent sure thing."

"At least," Allegra said, "it *was*. You never know what's going to happen, do you? This is one of the more benign examples. Of course, I didn't make any commitment."

"Allegra!"

"So, don't worry. I didn't sign anything."

"Now, wait."

"But Brad tell me, how did you come to this decision? It's such a huge change!"

"Hang on, Allegra. I want to know what the DeVere had to say."

The DeVere.

All the time Mona had been in Vancouver she had been trying to get attention from a gallery like that, ever since she moved into sculptural form. Erica DeVere was the cream. She had earned a reputation for recognizing talent in young artists others might ignore, and she promoted what she believed in. Her people were regularly chosen for the Bienale, Munich, and other international exhibitions.

"Look," he said, "if Erica DeVere has already said she likes my work, well it's there, it's done. I've got at least enough for this one show."

"Oh, but...I'm not sure that would work. No unknown artist sells enough the first time even to pay for the cost of the show. So they're looking for someone serious, long term. I never should have gone ahead without your knowledge. I don't know what got into me. And now you're not going to like what I have to say. You're going to think it sounds insulting."

"No, of course I won't think that."

"If they took you on they'd see it as an investment—in your future as much as theirs. They'd be expecting you to expand your imagery, and grow."

"And you don't think I can do that?"

"Of course. I think you can do anything. But why would you get involved in all of that, especially if what you want to do is quit? What if you went on, and started emulating what other people think you ought to do? If you've decided to quit, I don't think you should let the offer of a show turn you around."

A show.

℘

Erica DeVere came around and saw the work. She came in a silver Jaguar. She wore silky clothes of beige and cream. She trailed the scent of Europe through his house, and her slight accent made him think of the chatter in sidewalk cafes, hooves on cobblestone streets, places he had never been.

Her gallery had had a cancellation, that was the reason she was able to give him this show. But it would have happened anyway; she owed a great debt to Allegra, she said.

It turned out that Allegra had taken slides of Brad's other drawings of herself as well, the secret ones; and these, above all, had impressed Erica DeVere. This work was truly remarkable, Erica insisted.

"Yes, of course it must be shown! Now, why don't you and I get down to terms?

During the weeks before the opening, Brad felt the most exhilarating terror of his life. On one hand, his mind was filled with possibilities he had never dared to imagine. Already, as he worked with Erica's assistant selecting canvases, deciding which drawings should be included, matted, framed, he could feel absolution from a whole range of petty failings.

On the other hand, he could no longer bring himself to paint at all.

<p>

During that period, Brad found himself going to Allegra's more than he had for quite some time. There was always something new he had to do. He was determined to make her small, high room function efficiently. She couldn't see what was good for her; she still had those layers of lumpy rugs, coat racks. He finished building her a room divider with floor-to-ceiling shelves on either side. Often she would be out when he came over, as it was months ago. These days it was to visit one of her doctors.

And, as usual, he was interrupted by the constant ringing of the phone. He let the call go onto the machine.

"Hello, it is DiSemele," a voice Brad vaguely recalled said. "I have needed to be out of town for a long trip. But now that I am returned, I have good news for you."

He left a number. *I have good news for you.* Probably someone calling to see her silk, not aware her printing business had died. The message would just stir up old longings and regrets. Better she didn't know. He pushed delete. After he finished the room divider, he fixed the plug on her VCR.

It was soothing, during those weeks, to spend time in her rooms. His own house was full of dead things, expiring canvases, piles of drawings that sometimes stirred. On long nights he stared at what he had created, in futile search of an antidote. Something was wrong with them, and that was keeping him from painting. Often he went into the bedroom and stared into the mirror. As a boy he had looked and looked in his mother's mirror, wondering if his face gave away his rotten core.

Dimly he could recall the sense of relief he had felt just before he had heard Allegra's news, relief that the effort of having to dredge his emotions could cease, that if it had the grace to leave you, it was best to let it go.

April

*I*t is human folly, this desire to catch the eye of fortune, and equally ingrained is our urge toward excess. Think of that famous meeting among royalty in the Middle Ages which became known as the Field of the Cloth of Gold, for the manner in which that fabric draped every surface: the horses, the stage, the royal thrones, entire banquet halls, the shoulders of the kings.

This was not the first time a weight of gold fell upon a king.

The wine god Dionysus enters here. Though he was the god of revels, he had also spent years as a lonely wanderer. He had been orphaned as a child, or rather snatched up by his father, Zeus, when his mother, Semele, made the fatal mistake of asking to see the god in his radiant other-wordly form. The mother of Dionysus died in that burning light.

The oldest friend of Dionysus was Silenus. One day this amiable old drunk fell asleep beside the road. Those who found him mocked him, tied him up in garlands, took him along to King Midas of Phrygia, thinking this was a great joke. But Midas welcomed him as an honoured guest.

It pleased Dionysus, to see his old friend honoured in this way. He told Midas he would grant him any wish he asked.

"I wish that everything I touch would turn to gold."

He hardly dared believe it, as he wandered out into the sunlight. He thought perhaps this encounter with the god had been a dream. Idly he reached out and picked a twig from an oak tree. The leaf stiffened, the twig snapped with a quick metallic sound. He was staring at a leaf of gold.

He picked up a pebble from the ground, and instantly it became heavy as a stone, its small dense shape giving off a brilliant yellow gleam. He clutched at a clump of grass, and in his hand he held a bundle of thin glinting spears. He reached for an ear of corn, suddenly hungry—but no, what he held was "a heavy slug of gold...its grains inedible, inaccessibly solid with the core." He frowned. He reached for a juicy apple on a tree, and immediately understood that he would break his teeth on gold.

℘

On the afternoon of Brad's opening, Allegra took a long time to get into her silk flower-printed dress, a flowing whispy creation in lilac and burgundy and cream, which she had bought in a thrift shop back in the early Seventies. She had never worn it. She examined her face closely in the mirror. Three times she had needed to stop and re-do her makeup, the lipstick smearing, or the mascara feathering her cheek.

It was hard to remember what she had hoped to accomplish

when she'd forced Brad's work out into the world. Certainly she'd hardly thought about his fears. Her heart clenched for him now.

Erica had pulled out all the stops. Posters were up all over town, and there were ads in both the local papers and even in the weekend *Globe*. A woman in a red dress, dancing wildly: *The Allegra Series: Brad Lindhall, Recent Work*. Yes she had agreed to lend her name. Hadn't this all been her idea?

When Brad arrived to pick her up she said, "Look at you. You look wonderful." He was wearing brown cord pants she had never seen before, and a chamois-looking shirt. Nicky was with him. Nicky handed Allegra a box containing a gardenia.

"And look at you!" Allegra said. Nicky had on jeans and blinding high-cut sneakers, and a windbreaker. "Mom bought me these," Nicky said pointing to his shoes. "She's coming tonight. She's coming to Dad's show."

Allegra lied and said, "I know."

§

But surely that could not have been the reason she had decided not to go—the picture of herself pushing a waist-high path through a room full of conversation, wearing her grandmotherly corsage, while beautiful people peered from her to the stunning face of Mona and from Mona to Allegra's many representations on the wall.

She did have a pounding headache. Brad did not argue long.

"So, go on," she said, "you're going to be late. Phone me. Let me know how it is going!"

She sat in her apartment, imagining how the gallery would be buzzing with exclamations and questions: "But who is the woman in the mirrored tower?" She pictured Erica DeVere presiding in her regal pseudo-friendly way, and by her side, her companion, who reminded Allegra of a Russian wolf-hound: narrow face, eyes close-together, haughty dim intelligence.

When the phone rang, her heart rose and fell. She uttered a quick prayer that all was going well.

"Allegra!" It was Faye, her voice gone shrill because of all the background noise. "What's going on? You should be here! The whole town's here."

"So it's going well?"

"You didn't tell us his work was this good!"

Allegra felt an inner heave, like riding out an ocean swell. "All of it? You like it all?"

"I will say this: it has made you a star. Though it's just too bad about that nasty incident earlier. That was my favorite painting, too!"

"I don't understand."

"Oh." Faye said. "I assumed you'd already heard."

ø

Midas strode toward his palace, absently touching the pillars of his porch as he passed through. Yellow marbled up through the stone, and then all was shining, flat with the glare of gold.

Concerned now, he tried to wash his hands in the courtyard fountain, thinking to dilute this gift a bit. The water "coiled into the pool below as plumes of golden smoke, settling heavily in a silt of gold...."

Now he began to sweat. Desperate with hunger, desperate for drink, he sat at his table. His servants brought out fine meats and fruit and bread. He reached for a roast chicken, and stared at what might have been a gleaming ornament, gold drumsticks, gold breast, gold rippled skin, little gold tucked-under wings. He reached for bread that would not break. In terror, but keeping his actions deliberate he reached for his goblet of wine, carefully pouring in water to mix with it. He sipped, and his companions saw him "mouthing gold, spitting gold mush...that had solidified like gold cinders." He rose from his gold chair and threw himself face-down on his gold divan, the folds of the pillow gouging his cheek.

Now he prayed to have this gift taken from him. And Dionysus, tired of the joke or lesson, told Midas how to wash the gift away in a certain river that flowed down past the city of Sardis. That river carries traces of gold dust to this very day.

℘

What Faye told her, Allegra could barely comprehend. The show had been a sensational success right from the start, a large (wealthy) crowd flowing in, eager to see Erica's latest protégé, despite the occasional whispers from those who declared his work was overexcited, gauche, the work of a novice getting more attention than he deserved. Red SOLD stickers started to bloom on the walls.

Then Mona arrived.

"I hardly recognized her," Faye said. "She has shaved her head. She is as bald as an egg. She came in so solemnly, all dressed in white, like a priest— huge baggy pants and a high-necked shirt, but with a strap across her shoulders that held something hanging in a sheath, the way a soldier might wear a sword—and black boots, which gave her a very clumping measured stride. She was such a presence that the whole place hushed as she walked around and looked at painting after painting."

"But I don't understand," Allegra said. "Didn't she come with Brad?"

"No, Brad looked alarmed. I think *everyone* was alarmed, though we didn't quite know why. It was like a collective premonition; everyone froze. Then she stopped in front of one of the paintings and pulled a pair of enormous scissors out of the sheath and she stabbed the painting, slashing the canvas to ribbons before anyone could move. It was the one with a lake and the woman on the hilltop standing with her arms spread like wings. Do you remember that one? Allegra?" Faye's voice seemed very distant now. "Allegra, are you there?"

"What happened then?" Allegra finally managed to say. "What happened to Mona? And how is Brad?"

"Oh, it was amazing, really. The whole thing only caused a momentary blip in the buzz of the crowd. Though I do remember the flash of a camera. That reporter from *The Sun* was there so I expect tomorrow it will be on the front page. But the place is humming now. I've never seen an atmosphere like this at an opening. I'd say three quarters of the show is sold! You've got to come. Don't worry about Mona. I think Brad took her home. So why don't I come over and pick you up? It's your show, Allegra. You should be here."

ဢ

"Do you remember that one?" Allegra barely managed to pour herself a glass of the cherry brandy. She spilled half of it down the front of her dress. She drank what remained in one long gulp, the stickiness of what she'd spilled soaking through between her breasts. Did victims who were stabbed also feel this need for sweetness? She became

conscious of the wind straining against the windows, the low sky hurling rain, the darkness pressing in.

She was a ghost, no longer there, no longer anywhere. She passed by, floating whisps of pity, shreds of terror.

§

It would be comforting to think that Midas had learned something useful. He certainly learned to scorn the lure of gold. He left his palace for a time and went to live a simple life in the fields and forests. Perhaps he thought that having left behind the carefully ordered palace life he had also dispensed with the need for diplomacy: as if a diet of roots and vegetables bestowed the virtue of frankness. Besides, he still was King.

When he chanced upon a music contest in the woods between the great god Apollo, and the small god Pan, Midas refused to agree with the judges, who had declared that the mighty sun-god (at any moment capable of withdrawing his light) was the more talented musician. Apollo—piqued, but judging this small king hardly worthy of a major punishment—made a passing gesture as he departed, which turned the king's ears into those of a donkey.

Midas slunk back to his palace and covered his head with a purple hat, determined that no one would know. But even a king needs to get his hair cut. When that time came, Midas swore his barber to secrecy, promising to disembowel him if he talked.

The secret swelled in the barber, but he dared not tell a soul. Still, he had to get rid of it. One night he crept from the palace and dug a hole in the ground. Kneeling, he whispered, "Midas has asses' ears." Relieved to have said the words, though no one heard, he covered the hole, stamped the earth and went away. But a clump of whispering reeds sprung up there, almost over night, and with every gust of wind they whispered the words the barber had buried beneath their roots. "Midas has asses' ears, Midas has asses' ears." Soon every wind in the country carried the news.

§

Brad led Mona into the office at the back of the exhibition space, conscious of too many people pressing even here. He thought he would need to calm her down, but she was as expressionless as someone in a trance. He took her home. He felt in a trance himself. His head was filled with the sound of ripping canvas, gasps of indrawn breath, the impression of clouds of rising dust, shattering glass, as if an explosion had taken place.

Brad put Nicky to bed. "Why did Mom do that?" Nicky asked.

"It's complicated. Shh. She'll tell you in the morning."

"Will she still be here?"

"Yes, of course."

Then Mona came in, and she lay with Nicky for a while. She sang him the whole of Yellow Submarine.

"What kind of song is that?" Brad heard his son's overtired voice demand.

"Do you want a song or not?"

"But could we do that?" he asked when she had finished. "Could we all go in a submarine, you and me and Dad?"

She sang the song again.

Brad sat in the kitchen. There was a bowl of fruit on the kitchen table. The bowl was from Allegra's studio, and most of the fruit was too, but in among the glazed approximations were some real apples.

Mona came from the bedroom and stood in front of the sink, on the old hooked rug.

"You know, that was rape, that night," she said looking at the rug.

Brad took an apple. He remembered how his mother used to cut an apple when he was sick, so the halves made shallow bowls, their flesh scooped out with a spoon.

Mona had conceived a child and kept the child and carried the baby to term. She hadn't said no. She had let him get down on his knees. When she had finally tried to push him away, he had just covered up her mouth with his mouth. She had never mentioned it once in all these years. He took a knife and cut the apple he was holding. The flesh was crisp and streaked with pink, and the core made a star that held the seeds, and some of those seeds were sliced right through.

He said, "That was a terrible thing to do. How could you do that? Don't you know Allegra isn't well? What do you think that will do to her?"

"Allegra! Oh my god. That wasn't about Allegra."

"What do you mean?"

"That is so typical," Mona said, "that just proves how you will never have even the remotest idea of where I'm coming from. To put that down to jealousy."

She was glaring at him. What nerve she had. He had forgotten what this was like. She might be crazy, though she didn't look it anymore. She looked like Mona as he had always known her, as he had fallen for her years ago in the art school. He'd passed through the cafeteria with his box of tools and seen a woman so spiky he knew that somehow or other he was going to have to touch her. It was all he could do now to keep from reaching out and cupping the pale smooth globe of her head with his hands.

"What was it about then?"

"It was performance art, of course. Didn't you see the whole thing being filmed on video?" She said this with a serious face.

"What sort of performance was it supposed to be?"

"It's based on the myth of Philomela. You wouldn't understand."

"No, you're right. I wouldn't understand." He grabbed her wrist.

"But I forgot about Allegra," Mona said. "I was so furious with you, when I learned you were painting. It's called Vengeance. The piece. It will run at my next installation, along with some other ones I'm working on. I'm sorry about your painting. You have to understand that for this to work it required real emotion, real living sacrifice. But I wasn't thinking of Allegra, at all. I should call her now. I should explain."

"Oh Christ," Brad glanced at his watch.

It was not too late. Allegra would still be waiting.

"Better not," he said. "She will be sound asleep by now."

"I should send her a letter, tomorrow then. I think that would be better, anyway. I could explain, and send her some of the stills. She would be interested don't you think?"

Brad had imagined, for so long, that Mona's presence ran in counterpoint under all of his other thoughts, even of Allegra, even of his art. Now he was remembering how she was like water, its clarity suddenly riffled into patterns by the wind, changeable, utterly provoking, provocative. The way she looked at him, setting the whole question of Allegra easily aside, she knew he'd reach for her.

"Oh," she said not much later. "I have been celibate for so long." Was this a performance, too? Should he be listening for the whir of the video?

℘

April

We live and breathe and disappear. Who keeps our stories? Who kept the stories even of the gods, before the written word? Their feats were recorded by their mythical offspring in woven cloth; later we know from Pliny and Pausanias that the walls of Athens were covered in murals that told heroic tales. Yet the fabric has crumbled, the walls have fallen, the murals have disappeared. The ancients carved stories in ivory too, and wood. Now dust. Most of the gold and silver and bronze has been melted down, the words inscribed there pooling into ingots, household vessels, coins.

Clay is what is left. The painted vases of the Greeks, which may be the greatest treasure-trove of ancient story.

Greek vase painting began after the dark age that followed the mysterious destruction of the Mycenaean world. At first the decoration was mainly geometrical. Then came the scenes of myth, a burst of story-telling that lasted well into the Hellenistic times. These vessels survived because clay is without inherent value. It cannot be melted down. It is unlikely to decay. A vase broken in many pieces can still be reassembled. Yet many have come down to us unbroken, thanks to civilizations like that of the Etruscans which valued them greatly and placed them in tombs—where they were passed over by looters in search of artifacts and adornments in precious metals, remaining perfectly intact for centuries....

§

When the phone rang the day after the opening, and Mona picked it up, the caller hung up right away. Brad knew who it was. He knew it was despicable, the way he did not call Allegra back: not the next day, or the one after, or even after Mona had finally left for Toronto. Eventually this neglect became so unforgivable he realized *she* must be the one to blame.

She could have called him back. Not one word did he hear from her about his show. She might have known he would be worried about her reaction. By keeping silent she was screaming. He began dwelling on what puzzled him: that incident at the studio, then the surprising business of arranging the show, though he had sworn her to secrecy. He'd given almost a year of his life to an unstable stranger.

For after a little while, after quitting his job and taking time to go camping with Nicky, and after starting to get a hint of what it could be like to be free, he saw that he had been living Allegra's life, both inside his art and out of it, all that time. But now his life had turned. Erica had sold almost his entire show, and she expected much new work from him.

§

A vase unearthed in Italy, in the middle of the nineteenth century, now known as the François vase, is one of the few that tell the story of Ariadne.

A frieze on one side shows the Cretan princess being honoured by the troop of Athenian youths and maidens who have joined hands and are dancing towards her. She faces them holding a wreath and a ball of yarn, accompanied by her nurse. In the background is the many-oared boat in which she will shortly sail away with Theseus.

On the other side of the vase she stands facing Dionysus in a stance that some experts in iconography say presents a clear parallel with Aphrodite. Thus it may be assumed that in the mind of the painter of this vase, and therefore in the ethos of the time when it was made (about 570 B.C., signed by the potter Ergotimos and the painter Kleitias), the figure of Ariadne had a close association with the goddess of love.

This may help lay to rest rumours that later floated around the Aegean world, even finding their way eventually into twentieth century literature.

April

One morning Brad woke up early, and could not get back to sleep. Nicky had stayed over at his grandparents' place the night before. The house was too quiet. He got up and made himself some coffee, and pulled on his clothes. Perhaps a drive. He headed out to his van.

Once he'd crossed the bridge, the building complex with Allegra's apartment was almost directly to the left. He veered to the right before he'd even thought it over, cut across to Seymour, heading in the opposite direction. That was how he found himself on East Cordova, at FibreWorks' old studio.

He'd always hated this part of town. She didn't understand the east end of the city as he did. She used to try to tell him about the people she met down here, drunks who staggered up the alley and peered in the back door.

"They all think they could have been artists," she said, "and I'm sure many of them could still be. I would love to open up some sort of communal studio for them. A worthy project, when I'm rich."

The night before he had been at a dinner party given by a woman who had bought two of his large paintings. This was at a house designed by a Vancouver architect with an international reputation. A long low house on the hill above Spanish Banks, room flowing into room, a sweeping view across to the north shore where mountains gleamed in the setting sun. Before dinner the guests drank champagne poured from green bottles decorated with small white flowers. They stood and drank and chatted out on a terrace above a slope of rhododendrons coming into bloom. They nibbled prawns and scallops dipped in saffron mayonnaise. Erica DeVere was there, with her friend Knut who sold antiques, and a couple of middle-aged lawyers with their young and gleaming second spouses, who were lawyers too and of course the host and hostess who were charming, intelligent, old, astoundingly energetic, and very wealthy.

His hostess had a passion for music as well as art. At dinner she regaled them with tales about the city in its musical infancy. There were many stories involving people Brad had never heard of, but he smiled when a smile was called for. His hostess had seated him on her left and she waved her arm in his face. The beauty of this arrangement was that he hardly had to say a word.

Brad's head was buzzing by the end of the evening. Tuscany, the Middle East, cruises down the Nile, between them the people around the table had been several times around the world. As for the world of art, they were all significant collectors. Now Erica intended that they begin collecting *him*.

He had an exceptional hangover, this morning. FibreWorks was still there. Closed of course, at this hour. He found himself pulling up in front.

There was pottery in the window, and some weaving. Whoever was running it was obviously taking in work on consignment. From inside the shop, he could hear the din of the burglar alarm.

He stood on the sidewalk, resisting venturing up the narrow, reeking stairs to the hotel above. "Anyone there?" he shouted, "Anyone in charge?"

"All right, sir, that's okay."

A man clattered down. He had a face like papier-maché.

"She's coming to turn her off." He gestured up the stairs. "I'm just going out to get her coffee. She'll be down to turn it off in a few minutes." She.

May

*T*he story of Ariadne starts with Europa, her grandmother, who caught the attention of Zeus when she was gathering spring buds and was carried off by him to Crete. There Europa gave birth to three sons, Minos, Rhadamanthys, and Sarpendon, who grew up under the care of the Cretan king.

The eldest boy Minos eventually succeeded to the throne. He took as a wife a woman of perfectly decent lineage (the sun-god was her father) by the name of Pasiphae. She had two daughters. The elder was Ariadne.

Now, Poseidon decided to honour Minos by sending him a remarkable white bull to sacrifice. This wondrous animal emerged roaring and snorting from the sea. Unfortunately Minos could not bring himself to kill such a magnificent creature. He kept it for himself. As punishment, Poseidon inflamed the queen with such monstrous passion for the bull that she begged the great artist

Daedalus to make her a hollow cow, so she could satisfy her lust. The Minotaur was the result. She gave birth to a monster with a man's body and the head of a bull, who fed on human flesh. To hide the disgusting thing, King Minos built the Labyrinth beneath his palace. Then he demanded tributes from all his vassal states. Every year one or another of them had to send seven youths and seven maidens to be fed to the Minotaur. Athens had to supply its tribute every seven years.

That was how Theseus came to Crete. The young prince of Athens swore to his father that he would go as one of the sacrificial youths, and slay the Minotaur or die. And that is how he met the princess Ariadne.

§

During the weeks that followed his show, Brad admitted only stray thoughts about Allegra. Erica was pushing him; he had plunged into a frantic, heroic burst of work for a show in six months time, this one to open simultaneously in Vancouver and Toronto. The subject matter had come to him while he was camping with Nicky. Aspects of Rape. He was concentrating on landscapes of clear-cuts, balding hills, eroded gullies, charred and blackened stumps. Though the subject matter was bleak, Erica was enthusiastic about the early drawings.

When he was buying art supplies one day he ran into Faye Minot in the market on Granville Island. He hardly recognized her at first. Her hair was cut in a brush-cut; she was wearing an untucked red-and-white Hawaiian shirt and white lace-up shoes. Faye avoided any mention of Allegra and so did he.

Later that same day when he stopped in at the gallery to pick up the payment for the final pieces from his show, Erica remarked (as she wrote the cheque with a small firm hand that hefted a square emerald set in a bezel of old-fashioned gold) "Ah, what a shame about our dear friend," as if he would know exactly what she meant. She smiled over the rim of her half glasses as she handed him the cheque. "But it would have been a burden for you, in any case, when you have so much to do."

He drove home through the grey rain. He was soaked by the time he got into the house. He towelled off and went back to work on a drawing of upturned stumps, the severed roots waving like arms and legs.

§

On the night before the youths were sent to the Minotaur, Minos entertained Theseus and his companions lavishly at the palace. During the banquet Minos quizzed Theseus about his exploits, and mocked the prince's claim to be the son of the god Poseidon. "Here," he said (they were sitting on a terrace high above the sea) "if you are the son of Poseidon, fetch back this ring for me." He took a ruby from his finger and threw it into the sea. Theseus leapt to the railing and dove down into the wine-dark water. When he surfaced, he carried not just the ring, but the golden crown of the sea nymph Thetis. Ariadne fell in love.

We know some of what followed. How Ariadne guided Theseus to the centre of the labyrinth and out again, on the promise that Theseus would take her back to Athens and make her his queen. And how, when his ship arrived in Naxos, he abandoned her.

This is where the rumour starts. Some say that in Crete vestiges of the ancient worship of the Earth Mother lingered on into the time of Minos and that Ariadne had been the secret High Priestess of this cult in which a king was chosen for a yearly reign—only to be sacrificed at crop time. Whispers have implied that on Naxos she reverted to the ancient savage rites, joined the maenads in their orgy, participated in the yearly slaughter of the king.

This is without basis in either myth or art.

What we do know from two thousand years of story is that Theseus left her alone on the island, in the night—possibly, as some say, fearing to take a stranger home as his wife—possibly smitten by the gods, as others say, by a strange and cruel forgetfulness. He carried on, in any case, with what he would believe was a better love with the Amazon Hippolyta: never recognizing that the slaying of the Minotaur had only been the start, that what he had held so briefly in his hand was the thread to his true worth.

Then the god Dionysus came and found Ariadne weeping. Tigers and lynxes drew the chariot in which he rode, and a band of fauns and satyrs danced around, their loose hair wreathed in ivy leaves. Dionysus had compassion for the beautiful princess. He loved her and he made her his wife.

Zeus granted Ariadne immortality then, and Dionysus set her bridal crown among the stars.

℘

One day when Brad emerged from a long morning of work, he found a letter in the brass box by the door. He recognized Allegra's hand on the envelope, though the writing was childlike. On the back, he saw her old address had been applied with a rubber stamp.

The card inside had a picture of a cow wearing shiny biker glasses. I have to see you, she had scrawled. Nothing more.

He replied, also by note, setting up a date in ten days time, unless he heard back the contrary, he said.

All week long he was flooded by one memory, then another. Opening a tin of beans, he saw Allegra toying with her food, heard her telling him about her mother who ran off with a man who rode Brahma bulls. Adding up his cheque book he remembered her passion for calculations, puzzles. Tying a shoelace he recalled her tapestry: "I've been wanting to tell you what this is about, for so long," she had said a few days before his show, opening the cupboard door, revealing the tapestry he'd caught a glimpse of long ago.

"No, you won't make much of the design. It's all symbolic, but Angeline will understand. I met someone who said he would help me find her. I don't know what happened. He never called."

How infinitely long it must have taken her to work a small block of colour.

℘

Her door was ajar. She was waiting by the window in her motorized chair. She wore a whitish floating dress, something the evening light filtered through. Her hair was the same. Her skin was the same. He had forgotten the clarity of her.

"Hi," she said. "It's good to see you," as if this were any ordinary call. "Actually, before you sit down, there's some wine over there."

He looked around the room. Not much had changed. The tall cupboard stood open. The tapestry was no longer hanging behind the door. Her coat-trees had grown a second crop of handbags and various sorts of outer wear. The table was taken over by a computer.

"Oh, someone found me that," she said. "I'm into something exciting."

The phone rang. While she hesitated, Brad heard her familiar message click on. She reached out quickly to turn down the sound.

She crossed to the computer and flicked it on. It wheezed and blips of light flickered on the screen. Brad knew that when they got this old you paid people to take them off your hands. A couple of seconds went by before the screen settled down.

"There is a cosmologist at Princeton who has a theory about cosmic strings," she said. "He believes there are sheaves of energy left over from the Big Bang and that these could allow us to discover short-cuts through space and time."

This was not going the way he had expected. He thought he had been dreading a scene. Now he saw that he had been dreading this, that she would reach for his hand and pull him down beside her, that he would watch her fumbling over the keyboard, see incomprehensible figures stacking up against blue infinity—that he would follow all the same, hypnotized and willing, through the gap she made in space and time.

He pulled away, fetched the bottle and the glasses, took them over to the coffee table where she had been sitting.

"How can you stand that?" he said.

"What do you mean?"

"It's not very practical."

She looked quizzically at him as she turned off the computer and rolled back across the room.

"I've had it with practicality. On Mondays I see a Chi-Gong master. On Wednesdays I go to my hypno-therapist. On Thursdays I research chemical poisoning. Do you know people all over North America have mysteriously fallen sick? I believe it may be at the root of my illness."

She maneuvered to the spot by the window, over uneven hills of patterned rugs.

"And then the studio lumbers on. Jim has taken it over. I put him in touch with some artisans. He's handling other lines and the place is actually hobbling along. Is that practical enough?

"You know my fascination with pattern, design. Well, just when every other pathway seemed closed to me, I find I can use a computer. And with it..." she shook her head as she recognized how hopeless this would be to explain. When she lifted her glass he saw that he had filled it too full.

"But *you're* not doing all that well, are you? You weren't always so bleak. You're not happy with your work? Is that it?"

"No, my work's going well. I've just started a new series on an environmental theme."

"Oh yes?"

"Actually I've gone off on a tangent about garbage, recently. I took a lot of photos at the recycling depot and I'm working those into drawings."

She considered this. "Yes, I can see that garbage would offer a wealth of patterns." He saw that she really could. "All those tins, with just a touch of variation, some squashed, some with jagged lids...."

She took hold of his hand, spread it on her palm. She traced the top of it, the knuckles, the veins.

"You know, I think they read the wrong side of hands. I think you can tell more about a person by their knuckles. Look at that, you've got the hand of a good person." She folded it and handed it back to him. "Of course, I asked you over because we have some unfinished business, don't we?"

Behind her Brad could see the traffic on the bridge, strings of cars moving in each direction. In the mirror on the balcony he could see ships bobbing in the inlet, and some sail boats, three of them, and a wind-surfer, too, though dusk was closing in. It was starting to rain.

Those eyes. So green, flecked yet clear.

He looked away, at the floor. All her carpets, wrinkled, overlapping. Living. The word puffed and slimmed in his head like a fish beneath the sea, following its own watery trails. He did not know why he should be sitting in this room, glassed-in, dusk rising, as if this were the only place life was swimming through.

His reply sounded like so many knocks on a block of wood. "I guess we do."

She rubbed her forehead, tried to clear loops and strands. "I don't think people should just slip out of each other's lives. I think our lives need punctuation. Small ceremonies. Gifts of courtesy."

He ran his finger round and round the rim of his wine glass. A glass from Mexico, green and chunky. His finger pulled out no singing note at all.

"So I guess you've been seeing someone else," he said.

"That's not the point. Yes, and no."

"Someone who'll take care of you, I hope."

She laughed. "Let's say I've had some good news. I won't go into all of that right now." She had been fingering her locket, and now she let it fall inside the neck of her blouse. "I just needed to see you before I leave."

"Leave?"

"Erica didn't tell you? That's interesting."

"Leave, for where?"

"Oh, off to one of the islands. There's a place out there." She gestured toward the gulf.

"What place?"

She narrowed her eyes. "I don't think it's a place you would approve of. The director has established centres of alternative medicine all around the world. There was an article in the paper not long ago: the healing properties of cabbages, a particular kind of grape, foxgloves. Yes I know," she laughed and wobbled her hands in the air. "But I have to take this chance."

Foxgloves. He saw himself with Mona, rutting on the floor. It was what she had wanted when she was back: the worst part of himself, played out again and again.

"When are you going?"

"Probably quite soon. I've just got to figure out what to do with my things."

When he'd been working on his drawings this afternoon, Brad had felt that he understood what his work was all about, finally. It was about paying attention, rendering that attention visible. Why, now, should he be looking back on his afternoon's work, his whole month's work, with the same feeling he'd had when he'd come to the end of the funnels?

Rain pounded against the window. The room was almost dark. He could hardly make out Allegra's face.

"I don't think you should go."

"What do you think I should do?"

"I want to look after you," he said.

She was shaking her head. "It would be much too hard."

"Look, Allegra, I'm doing well these days."

"I mean, too hard for me." She reached forward and took his hand again. "I had to talk to you before I went, because I don't want anything hanging over us. But now I'm going off into a life that has no need," she broke off, searching, then gave up, "for that kind of energy. Do you see?"

And now in the half dark, yes, he could half see. She was

dealing half in truth, half in lies, just as he was. Her gauzy dress held the failing light around her as she sat in her chair. She would always gather light. And he had not been paying attention, after all. Everything was the reverse of what he had believed. He saw the chalky curve into the narrow dark, the way he had used that shape, again and again, to train a circle of brightness on her life, from on high. He saw himself—touched, enlivened, part of the Allegra Series—falling through.

Acknowledgements

Of the many books that have been helpful and inspiring in the writing of this novel, I must mention particularly: *Women's Work, the First 20,000 years—Women, Cloth, and Society in Early Times*, by Elizabeth Wayland Barber, (W.W. Norton & Company, New York, London, 1994); *Weaving, a handbook for Fiber Craftsmen*, by Shirley E. Held (Holt, Rinehart and Winston, New York, 1973); *The Pleasures of Pattern*, by William Justema, (Reinhold Book Corporation, New York, Amsterdam, London, 1968); *A Merchant of Prato*, by Iris Origo, (Knopf, New York, 1957) quotes of which appear on pages 117-120, and 143-144; *Men and Gods*, by Rex Warner, (Penguin, 1950) quoted on page 125; *Tales from Ovid*, translated by Ted Hughes (Farrar Straus Giroux, New York, 1997) some quoted phrases from which appear on pages 47, 55, 68, 74, 75, 168, 170 and 171; and Mary M. Innes's translation of the whole of Ovid's *Metamorphoses*, (Penguin Books, 1955).

I thank *Canadian Fiction Magazine*, *The Malahat Review*, and *The Journey Prize Anthology* for publishing my work, and Marlene Cookshaw of *Malahat* in particular for her friendship and encouragement.

I thank my parents, the artist-potters Adolf and Louise Schwenk, for bringing me into their world where hard times never managed to crowd out creativity, and for giving me the lasting gifts of a love of art and myth. I thank Shaena Lambert for her faith in this story, her advice and her many insights; James and John Lambert for their wise comments; Lorna Schwenk for her beautiful drawings; Jamie Evrard for inspiring enthusiasm, for reading many drafts, and for sharing so much information about the rigours and rewards of an artist's life; Kathleen Conroy for reading the manuscript in various phases and for her honest and valuable thoughts. I thank my agent Carolyn Swayze for her guidance, astuteness and good humour. I thank Joy Gugeler, my editor at Beach Holme, for her vision and knowledge and remarkable pruning and shaping skills. I thank my dear friend Linda for leading me into worlds within worlds within worlds. And I thank Douglas Lambert for his constant encouragement and support.